About the Author

This is Robert Zagar's debut novel. Prior to this, he ran an osteopathic practice in London for thirty-five years. As a nurse, he started a healthcare clinic in the jungles of Guatemala, and briefly danced professionally. Born in America, he has lived in London for forty years.

Little Red Dolls

Robert Zagar

Little Red Dolls

Olympia Publishers
London

www.olympiapublishers.com
OLYMPIA PAPERBACK EDITION

A CIP catalogue record for this title is
available from the British Library.

ISBN: 978-1-80439-065-8

This is a work of fiction.
Names, characters, places and incidents originate from the writer's
imagination. Any resemblance to actual persons, living or dead, is
purely coincidental.

First Published in 2023

Olympia Publishers
Tallis House
2 Tallis Street
London
EC4Y 0AB

Printed in Great Britain

Dedication

I dedicate this book to Mary Noel and Rudy Jr.

Acknowledgements

I am immensely grateful to Claudia Colladon, Liz Una, Paddy Sutton, Elizabeth Harcourt, Ruby Cowling, Kim Lavely, Jeff Nelson and Vicky Coghill for reading my early drafts and giving me encouragement and feedback. A special thanks to Debz Hobbs-Wyatt, my literary mentor from Cornerstones. To my wife, Sarah Allen, for her relentless grammatical corrections, and, finally, to the playwright Olwen Wymark who read my first short story many years ago and said, "This ain't bad."

Chapter 1

"Ah, this is it, Frankey," he said to himself. "This is it."

It was dark when Frank stepped out of the hunting lodge and closed the door. The cold morning air rushed at his face and made him catch his breath. He gathered himself up. He tightened the orange hunting jacket around his neck then adjusted his bow and arrows. His body longed for the warm bed he had just left. But this was the first day of hunting season and he wanted to be out deep into the woods before any other hunters. He knew there was one big buck in the area and he was going to get it.

Eight years ago, Frank and his friends had bought land and constructed a hunting lodge. The others had driven up to the lodge yesterday. Frank always arrived a day before them. This allowed him to warm the lodge and get food in. More importantly, it gave him time to get a feel for the woods. He wanted to know what the ground underfoot was like, and whether leaves were still on the trees. Also, the wind direction. All these factors and more were needed to calculate a successful hunting plan.

Frank always made sure he was free at this time in November. He ran his own plumbing business in the city. Six years ago, his wife, Rita, had given up on him. A few years later he met Jenny with her two young boys. Jenny understood Frank. She never made undue demands of him, especially this time of the year. They lived apart. He always left his dog with her at hunting season; dogs and deer didn't mix. And the boys loved having the dog with them. Jenny gave him space. He needed to spend a lot time and energy on his hunting and fishing. If she left him to it, he always came back to her. And his loving was good.

Frank looked out into the darkness and waited for his eyes to adjust. The cold was sobering his body. He and the other men had tucked into the whisky and cigars after dinner last night. The whisky had led to bragging, which led to more whisky and finally to betting on who would kill the biggest deer. The money wasn't important to him. Frank felt he was the only true hunter in this group. It was vital that he stalk and kill the biggest deer. It was his badge of honor. Frank had left them all sleeping under their quilts, with their hunting dreams, loud snoring, and odorous gases. He walked a few steps and looked back at the wooden lodge. It was set in a clearing, surrounded by pine. A thin line of grey smoke crept from the chimney. He turned, lowered his head and set off for the woods nearby.

A layer of freshly-fallen snow had covered the frozen ground overnight. His boots made a muffled crunching sound as he walked to the edge of the woods. He would now have to slow his pace, for the sound would easily be heard by the deer. Frank stopped and took a deep breath. This allowed the dry, cold air to race deep into his lungs. His mind and body tensed momentarily by the sudden influx of cold. His eyes began to water and then they closed. He opened his eyes. He was calm and alert. The night's debauchery had left him. He was ready to hunt.

The land the men had bought ran five miles east to west and three miles north to south. The northern two thirds of the land was forest and the southern portion was a swamp that fed into a small lake. Frank's plan was simple. The day before, he had left his truck on a side road at the other end of the woods. He would work his way to the base of the hill a mile away. Then he would climb up and follow the ridge, stopping at times to scan north into the tree-covered valley and to the south into the vast swamp with its reeds and bull rushes. This would take him most of the short winter's day to complete.

"Come on, Frankey Buck," he said to himself. "Let's go get that big one." He moved into the woods, making sure his steps were silent in the snow.

Chapter 2

Michael arrived a day before the funeral. He lay in bed and stared at the digital clock that glowed on the table next to him. The green neon numbers read 2.45. He rolled onto his back and calculated the time where he lived. In London, it would be 8.45. His lazy partner, Andrew, would still be in bed ignoring their cats' pleas to get up and feed them.

"Michael, darling," he'd say. "Those cats. Oh those bloody cats! Feed them or throw them out the window!"

Andrew was a writer and a critic. He said it was imperative that he got enough sleep so that he had the energy and vitality to mine his creative coal face every day. Michael had to go to his work early. He argued that creativity did not need such a cosseted life.

"Oh, love," Andrew would say, "my art is cerebral – thoughts and words. Yours is physical." Then he would curl up into the duvet and meekly ask if it would be possible if Michael could leave a warm cup of tea by their bedside before he left.

He thought a warm cup of tea and two more blankets would be nice right now. The budget Minnesota hotel that he had booked into turned its heat down at night. It was the end of November. He missed his partner's rotund belly to cuddle up to. He thought of sliding up behind Andrew in bed, kissing the back of his neck, and massaging his belly. After feeling Andrew stir, he would let his fingers move to his pubic hair and then finally to what Andrew called 'his old bear'. Michael became aroused. He thought of 'the old bear' and began to vigorously warm himself up. It ended in a muffled groan. He then fell back to sleep.

Michael left America ten years ago. He had arrived in a damp, rundown London with just two suitcases. At twenty-seven, he felt he had to make one final push in his dance career. In the early seventies, he had flourished as a male dancer in middle America. There was not much competition, and he moved quickly through the apprentice company to the main contemporary ensemble. There he toured through the local states from the artistic island of Minneapolis. They performed mainly in the university towns of Wisconsin, Iowa, and the Dakotas. Occasionally they would venture to Chicago or Denver. But mostly they danced in small, cold theaters in front of enthusiastic college audiences. Even though he was still young, his body was beginning to break down. Ankle, shoulder and back problems became a normal way of life. His real passion and talent was choreography. And this was his ticket out. Though he was good dancer, he knew he didn't have the talent to perform with the big New York companies like Merce Cunningham or Paul Taylor. In the summer of 1981, at a dance residence in Denver, a director of an English company liked his work, and proposed he come to London and work with her. The perfect storm of an injured body, dwindling arts funds, and breaking up with his boyfriend sent him across the Atlantic to work with Silvia.

Michael was woken by a hard knock at his door and a scurrying of feet. He jumped out of bed. The bedside clock read 6.04. He went to the door. "Hello? Hello? Who's there?" There was no response. He cracked the door and peered out. No one. He swung it wide open and saw an empty corridor. His bare foot trod on something small and soft. He recoiled and looked down. There on the floor was a small red doll with a brown bandana. Michael bent down and picked it up. He examined it closely. It was a little Indian doll in native dress with large, black, unblinking eyes. They were staring straight at him.

Chapter 3

The car park of the church began to empty. The cold of winter air made the cars cough and sputter as they navigated the ice under tire. Large drifts of glistening snow, like scoops of ice cream, had been pushed to the edges by snowplows. It made the cars look like they were surrounded by a snow castle. When the cars tried to move, they spun from side to side like drunken dancers. People behind the steering wheels leaned forward and peered through small portions of their defrosted windscreens. Blue grey exhaust billowed from each of the cars' tail pipes, filling the air within this castle.

In one corner of the car park, four cars were stationary. They huddled together closely like covered wagons in a Western. Some of the family stood outside the cars, while others warmed themselves inside.

"Christ Almighty," groaned Michael, as he dived deeper into his coat, exaggerating his shiver, "some people choose to live in this."

A cloud of freezing air seemed to encapsulate his words.

"Oh, you're such a pussy, Uncle Mike," Gina said. Gina was seventeen. Anne's only child. She mocked him, exaggerated his movements, and blew cigarette smoke in his direction. She wore a black leather jacket that covered her short, black skirt. The sharp heel of her high boots dug into the ice below her feet. The metal stud in her nose had a droplet of water on it.

Michael took his hands out of his pockets. He playfully took a couple of swings at her.

Gina stood to attention. She smirked and raised her fists. "Come on, old man. Make my day!"

He ducked and dived around her, making little stabbing motions. She giggled and blocked his attempts.

"Stop it, you two!" growled Anne. "All those people who are leaving can see you. This is a funeral. Remember?"

All the family were in agreement that Anne was born old and without a sense of humor. She was the second eldest of the four children. Anne bent down to pull up her surgical stockings from a recent varicose vein surgery. Gina and Michael raised their eyebrows at each other.

The family were told it would be an hour after the service before the priest would be ready to travel with them to the cemetery. It was decided to use the hall next to the church to serve a late breakfast for all those who came to pay their respects to Frank and the family.

This dull, unremarkable hall had history; it had been used to celebrate all their communions, confirmations, funerals and weddings. The ladies of the church had produced a mountain of ham, bacon, eggs, hash browns, pancakes, toast, and a lake of black coffee. The overpowering smell of cooked meat permeated the building. Gina, a vegetarian, stood outside with a piece of buttered toast and a cigarette. Inside, the overweight crowd jostled, chatted and consumed every last morsel of food. The ladies then efficiently cleaned the dishes and tidied the room while the rest of the congregation headed to their cars and home.

A snowball whizzed past Michael's head.

"Mom!" A boy of seven ran away from his older brother, who was pelting him with snowballs.

Michael turned and with outstretched arms moved towards

them. "Boys. Boys. Stop!"

The boys came to a sudden halt and spun around towards him. The older boy dropped his snowball on the ground.

Michael motioned to them, "Come here."

The boys glanced at each other, then strolled their way towards him. Although he wasn't their uncle, they knew he was Frank's brother. And they thought he sounded strange, coming from England.

"Boys, I know that's fun. Frankey and I used to do that a lot. I spent half of every winter brushing snowballs off me. Frankey was a great shot." He leaned over and put his arms around them. "Maybe we can have snowball fight later, me against you two?"

They nodded and ran off. Snowflakes began to tumble out of a grey sky like feathers from a burst pillow.

A short, stocky man with a thick black beard looked up at the sky. This was Marco, Anne's husband. "This doesn't look good. Anyone know the forecast?"

Mary stood next to him, shivering in her large green coat with its collar turned up and a black scarf wrapped around her neck. She was Frank's youngest sister. "It's supposed to be okay, just a little snow today." She tightened the scarf around her neck. "It will be freezing, though, the roads will be tricky." She lived in Florida now and, like Michael, didn't like this weather.

Marco looked at her shaking body. "You should get back into the car with your dad before you freeze to death."

She dipped her head and got back into her rented car.

The drive up to the cemetery would take two hours. They had the funeral early at nine so they could be on the road by eleven. It would be dark by four. After the service at the cemetery they still had to drive an hour to the hunting lodge, where they all would spend the night.

Marco pulled out a cigarette from his coat pocket and lit it. Anne tutted. He spoke before she had a chance. "I know I was supposed to quit, but this ain't the time."

Anne stared at him. She shook her head and walked away.

Other than the family, only two cars remained in the lot. One of them wouldn't start. The owner hunched over the open hood and attached a jump lead from the other car. Sparks flew into the sky as the slumbering car's engine was woken with the energy of another. There was a repetitive metallic grinding sound as the engine came to life. Finally, the engine ignited and roared.

"Ease off!" shouted the man under the hood. "You'll flood it!"

His wife, behind the wheel, took her foot off the pedal and the engine fell into a low, steady purr. The leads were put away. He thanked the other car's owner and then got behind the wheel as his wife moved over. Both cars made their way out of the lot.

Peter, Frank's father, watched the car's struggle through the back window of Mary's car. Through many long winters, he had started many people's cars. Never had his car ever stalled. His father had instilled a Germanic preparedness in him. Be ready, anticipate problems, never get caught out. He tried to pass this on to his children, especially his sons. Frank got the message. His younger son never did. Michael moved away from home as soon as he finished High School, while Frank stayed nearby.

Peter started to get impatient, as was his way. "When are we going?" he grumbled to no one in particular.

Mary turned in the front seat. "Soon, Dad. Soon."

Eventually the doors of the church flung open and through them hurried the priest and his small entourage. Dressed in a thick, black coat with matching gloves, scarf and hat, the portly Father Benedict resembled an ink dot rolling along the white carpet of snow. A young altar boy rushed ahead of him to open the rear door of the waiting car. Two older men followed behind carrying a pair of wooden boxes holding the urns of Frank's ashes. The priest got into the back seat. The boy closed the door behind him then got into the front seat next to the driver. The men opened the trunk of the car and placed the urns upon the floor. In the absence of a hearse, a small triangular blue and yellow flag flew from the antennae signifying a funeral. The gravesite was far from the church. The family were surprised that Father Benedict would accompany them to it. The priest told them that they were one of the founding families of the church, and he was honored to go with them.

Having seen the priest arrive, the family returned to their cars. A chorus of slamming doors filled the air. Branches of nearby trees shook; snow fell off them and startled birds took flight. The cars, led by the priest and Frank's ashes, left the car park and made their way onto the nearby highway. They lined up on the inside line to begin their journey north.

Chapter 4

"Hey, Frankey, how about you stop working and join us for a beer?" Jim said.

It was a summer's evening and the humidity was like a heavy, warm blanket. Horseflies buzzed in the air looking for humans to bite. Soon it would be the time for mosquitos to invade from the nearby woods.

When the men bought the land earlier in the year, they made a commitment to come and work on the property. They worked tirelessly on the weekends to build the hunting lodge. Now, after six months, it was completed. It was built with local pine, on the edge of a slope that overlooked a lake. Being on this incline allowed it to be constructed on two levels. The lower floor had four bedrooms in the back and an open area in the front for a pool table and television. Large glass doors opened to the lawn and down to the lake. The upstairs had two more bedrooms at the back. In the front, overlooking the lake, was a spacious open-plan kitchen, dining area and balcony. On the walls, stuffed deer heads were mounted. They looked out over the dining area in wild disbelief.

Frank finished his work and joined the group. The men sat around the wooden table in the lodge. Their shirts were drenched in sweat and their muscles ached from the day's labor. Plates of fried fish and bread were being eaten and washed down with ice-cold beer. The conversations were punctuated with laughing and deep bellied burps. Darkness was gathering outside. A crescent moon was rising over the pines. Soon the woods would be filled with dancing fireflies and the sky with stars. A gathering of crickets rhythmically buzzed outside on the lawn. Inside, the men were consumed by a gorged tiredness.

Some of the men spoke of going to bed early. At the end of the table, Matt, a burly salesman with short cropped hair, began to pound his fists on the table like a tom-tom. The other men yawned and quizzically looked at him. They stacked their dirty plates and returned to their conversations. Matt closed his eyes and pounded harder. The wooden table shook every time his fist hit the surface. He wasn't going to stop. Jim, a fat, balding accountant, ceased talking and joined in. The sound got louder. Bob and Jerry grimaced at each other and shrugged their shoulders. Then their fists hit the table in tandem with the first two. One by one, the other men stopped and picked up the beat with their clenched hands. They all closed their eyes. The rhythmical thumping sound completely filled the room and leaked out into the nearby forest. This continued for five minutes and the sound intensified. "Hey!" Matt shouted. He opened his eyes and jumped up. He threw his arms into the air and started to move around the table. The rest of the men did too, keeping the beat going by stomping their dirty boots into the floorboards. The mounted deer shook on the walls and looked on in horror. Frank was embarrassed by all this but tried his best to join in. The men shouted and whooped as they circled the table for another few minutes.

Matt stopped and procession came to a sudden halt. He punched the air. "Let's go!" he roared.

He burst through the doors to the balcony, down the stairs, and out into the night. The others shouted and hurried behind him. Wood was gathered and piled high near the shoreline. A fire was started and soon flames leapt into the black sky. Sparks burst like tiny rockets as the pine-sapped wood was heated by the fire. Soon, a massive bonfire was roaring. Matt motioned for the men to circle. The heat of the fire grew as the logs wildly popped and crackled. Matt threw his shirt off, and the others did the same.

"Yeah-Yeah-Yeah-Yeah!" they all chanted as they circled the fire.

Big Harry, who worked with cars, cried out, "Come on guys, let's do it!" He stopped, stumbled, and took off his boots and socks. He glanced at the men staring at him then ripped off his jeans and threw his underwear onto the bonfire. He spread his legs and raised his arms into the air. He thrust his head back and his glasses flew off his face. "Arrrrrr!" he bellowed.

They all laughed, hesitated and looked at each other. Then they did the same. Their jeans and underwear came off and were thrown to the ground. There was a momentary silence as they all stood naked in front of the blazing fire. Bits of ash floated into the night.

Jim, a fat, balding accountant, threw his arms up into the sky. "We gotta give ourselves hunting names!"

"Yes!" they shouted.

They all picked up dirt and rubbed it into their hairy bodies and faces. They hummed a tom-tom beat as they moved around the bonfire. These men had known each other since high school. They were fortunate that the Vietnam War was practically over by the time they were draft age. None of them had been damaged by war and battle. They played sports together. They dated the same girls. They had worked, married and had families all in the same unattractive, suburban town. This was a collective new beginning. Something that was a secret. Theirs alone. It was a chance to get back some life and create a new identity for themselves.

Jerry, a lean man with thick glasses, stopped and shouted to the stars, "From now on, call me Dark Bear!"

As they moved around the campfire, the other men came up with names for themselves. Harry became Red Fox, Bob named himself Full Moon, and Alex was Silver Spear.

Frank walked naked around the fire with the rest of them but was silent. He had needed these men to buy the land and build the lodge. But to him hunting and fishing were sacred; he didn't need any of this.

Jim turned to him. "Frankey, what's it going to be? Whatya going to call yourself?"

Frank looked at them all. They stood naked with dirt on their faces. "Guys, I don't know."

"Whatya mean, dunno?" Jim said.

"Come on Frankey!" Bob said. "Give us a name."

"Yeah!" the rest chimed in.

"Wait!" Jim raised his fist in the air, "I know what to call you. Frankey Buck. You shot that big son of a bitch last year. One bullet. One. Right in the heart. Frankey Buck it is!"

"Frankey Buck, Frankey Buck!" the others repeated.

In spite of himself, Frank smiled, pleased. "Okay, boys, Frankey Buck it is," he said.

Chapter 5

"You can sit wherever you want," said the waitress, "I will bring coffee and a menu over."

Michael found a corner table in the cafe and sat down. The cafe was part of the hotel where he was staying, and he was waiting to have breakfast with Mary. Sleepy, disinterested staff, mostly students from the nearby college, meandered through the tables trying to avoid the customer's eyes to take their orders. Their scuffling shoes scraped across the linoleum floor producing a high-pitched squeaking sound that irritated Michael's jet-lagged brain. He was tempted to tell them to pick up their God damn feet, but he restrained himself.

Mary came through the door. She scanned the room and their eyes met. Michael stood up and Mary, shyly dipping her head and shoulders, hurried over to him. He opened his arms and Mary buried herself into him, her head pushing hard into his chest.

"Hello, brother." Tears flowed down her cheeks.

"Hello, sister." Michael kissed the top of her head and tightly held her. Her rib cage moved in and out with short breaths. He pressed his lips again on the top of her head and this time he held them there. Her shaking subsided and she moved away from him and brought her hands to her eyes to brush her tears away.

"Dammit, Mikey," she said with a sheepish smile, "I promised myself I wasn't going to do that."

"Well, if you didn't, I would have." He wiped his eyes.

They stood for a moment looking at each other.

"Come, sit down." Mary sat down while Michael made a grand gesture with his arms. "Come, have breakfast with me here, at the Four Seasons restaurant, in Shady Oaks, Minnesota." Michael sat down. "This is where Rothko originally was going to hang a series of paintings," he said.

"Oh really?" Mary said with wide eyes.

"Absolutely. But he found the restaurant too commercial. He decided to hang them where they would be more appreciated. At the Tate, in London."

"Still the pretentious prick, I see."

Michael caught the eye of the waitresses and asked her for some coffee and menus.

Mary looked out at the snow-covered landscape. "Can you believe, Mikey, that we were born and raised here?"

"Don't knock it, honey, it is what made us. No soft, pampered life for us. We are self-made, with backbone."

"Yeah, right. You a fairy dancer and me a drug addict."

The waitress brought over menus and filled their coffee cups.

"And so. If this place gave such a solid platform in life, why did you leave it?" Mary asked.

Michael looked around and put a finger to his lips. "Shhh," he whispered, "damn right." He pushed a menu in her hand. "I hear the blueberry pancakes are good."

Mary glanced at the plastic menu while she pulled out a cigarette and lit it. The first puff covered the ceiling above them.

"Still on your cigarette diet, I see."

"Sure am."

"Well if you continue at the rate you are going, you'll disappear in a couple of months."

"Might not be a bad idea. Anything else? Doctor?" Mary took a couple more drags from the lipstick-tipped cigarette and then stubbed it out in the ashtray.

A thin, long-haired girl came over and stood over them with a paper and pencil in hand. "What would you like?" It seemed to take all the energy out of her, just to utter those words. Her eyes appeared closed. She looked like she might fall asleep on the spot.

"Pancakes!" Michael said, hoping to wake her up. "The blueberry ones. One stack for each of us. And bacon too. Please."

"Just one pancake for me and no bacon," Mary cut in.

"Nonsense! Give her the full works."

The girl stood over them with pencil poised, not writing anything. "I'm confused. What will it be?"

Michael glared at her. "As I said. A plate of pancakes and bacon for both of us."

His tone brought her to attention. She wrote down the order then turned on her heel. "Yes sir," she muttered, as she shuffled back to the kitchen.

"Thank you!" he snapped at her back.

Mary pulled out another cigarette. "That manner wasn't really necessary."

"I know. Sorry. Just a bit edgy. Not much sleep."

Another waiter came by and filled their coffee cups.

"How's Andrew?" Mary was the only one of the family to have visited Michael in Europe. In the ten years he'd lived there, she had been over three times. Not one of the rest of the family even had a passport.

"He's well. Sends his love. There's been a lot fear about AIDS." Michael stirred his coffee. "Four of our friends have it and it doesn't look good for them."

"You two okay?"

"Yes, we went together and got the test. It was a nervous few days before we got the results. We're both negative."

"That's great news!"

"Yes, we had a little party to celebrate. Just us two. Champagne, and the sex was brilliant," Michael giggled.

"That's enough information." She blew smoke out of the side of her mouth.

Michael briskly rubbed his face to try and wake up a bit more. He sipped his coffee. "Odd thing last night. I'd just fallen back to sleep when there was a knock at my door. No one was there. Someone had left a little Indian doll on the floor. Strange. Kind of spooky. Couldn't go back to sleep after that."

Mary stared at him then reached into her purse. "One of these?" She pulled out the same red doll with bandana and put it on the table between them.

Michael picked it up. "Yeah." He fingered its little arms and legs. "Exactly the same one. Was that you?"

Mary finished her cigarette. "No, it wasn't me. The same thing happened to me. A loud knock. No one there but for the doll. About six-thirty this morning." She stubbed the end of the cigarette into an ashtray. "I went to the reception and asked about it. They had no idea what I was talking about. It is not a gift. I asked two other guests at reception if they had gotten a doll. They hadn't."

"Think we're the only two that got these?" He looked at the doll. Then he put it back on the table. "Strange. What do you think?"

Mary picked up the doll. "No idea."

The pancakes and bacon arrived unceremoniously. Plates were dropped in front of them with a bottle of syrup. "Anything else?" the girl asked as she marched away.

Chapter 6

Three years earlier. April 1988.

Mary found a telephone booth in the main entrance to the hospital. She put a couple of dimes in the phone, dialed a number and listened to it ringing at the other end. Finally a sleepy voice answered.

"Frankey? It's Mary. I'm sorry to ring you so late," she said.

"Are you okay?" Frank's voice was bewildered, sleepy. "What time is it?"

"It's two in the morning," Mary said.

Frank's voice rose. "Where are you? What's happened?"

Mary winced at his anxious, loud voice. "Don't worry. I'm okay. I'm at the hospital. I need a ride home."

"Are you hurt? What time is it?" he asked again.

The phone started beeping, demanding more money. Mary hurriedly rummaged through her purse and found two quarters and shoved them into the coin slot. The beeping stopped and the line was clear again. "It's two in the morning, Frankey," Mary repeated. "No, I'm not injured." She burst into tears. "I got fired. They won't let me drive home."

"Fired? Christ, what happened?" Frank didn't wait for a reply. "Sure. Give me fifteen minutes and I'll be there."

Mary listened to him hang up and the line go silent. She hung up the phone and crumpled into a heap.

Mary worked the night shift and was the only nurse on a oncology unit. She had two young male medical students who served as orderlies for her. They did all the lifting and cleaning of the twenty patients while Mary distributed the medications. Even though she was only in her early thirties, her back was too fragile now to do any manual work. She had herniated a disc in her lower back three years ago, lifting an obese patient. Surgery had not been successful. She was left with an intermittent burning pain at the base of her spine that travelled deep into her right buttock. Physiotherapy and mild painkillers helped but sometimes the pain became all-consuming. And when it got really bad, Mary found a way to pull herself out the black web of pain.

The patients on this unit were terminal. Nothing could be done for them except make them more comfortable in their final days. It was essentially a hospice. Mary had taken the job and had been in charge of the unit for two years. Her previous supervisor was lazy. He slept most of the shift in his office. This allowed her to run the unit exactly the way she wanted. Every patient was cared for to the utmost. No one was ever neglected. She was proud of that. But she also used the situation to her advantage.

Edith Reed marched onto the ward with a clipboard firmly pressed against her chest. She was the new night supervisor. She was a tall, sturdy and serious woman. In her mid-fifties, her overuse of hairspray made her dyed-black hair sit upon her head like a dead beehive. Though she wore full glasses, she always perched them on the end of her nose. This allowed her to look you straight in the eye without any barrier. She examined the medication chart for the patients on the ward.

"I thought we agreed that you had to wait till I arrived before you administered the narcotics," she said.

Mary blushed. "I tried bleeping you but there was no reply."

She hadn't tried to bleep. She avoided eye contact with her supervisor, "Two of the patients were in real pain and needed something right away."

The large woman sighed. "Mrs. Jacobs, I'm not happy with this situation." She waited till Mary made eye contact with her. Their eyes locked. "I don't want to have to report you. But I will."

Mary's whole body bristled. "It's Ms. Breslin. And I said I tried to contact you."

They stood staring at each other. The beeping of the cardiac monitors could heard in the background. One of the orderlies was restocking supplies nearby. He lingered, listening in.

"Next time I will give you a written warning." Mrs. Reed surveyed her clipboard then glared at Mary again. "Let this be the last time." She turned and strode down the hallway.

Mary waited until her supervisor left the unit. Then she slipped into a side room and pulled out two vials of morphine from her nurse's uniform. These were the two that she said she had already given to the patients. She cracked the glass lids and drew up three equal doses into syringes. She checked to see what the orderlies were doing. One was dozing in the staff room, she couldn't locate the other. Mary hurriedly moved down the corridor and into the room of the two sleeping patients. She administered the drug via their intravenous catheters. Then she rushed to the toilet where she closed and locked the door. She sat on the toilet, pulled down her tights and injected the drug into her own thigh. In twenty minutes she would feel the warmth of the morphine. It would encase her in a soft, comforting cocoon. She would then be pain-free for the rest of the shift and glide effortlessly down the corridors of her work. This was her solution to the crippling pain that overwhelmed her; she took small amounts from each patient. She knew they were all over-medicated and taking a little from each wouldn't harm them.

They would still be pain-free and comfortable. She sat on the toilet seat for a few minutes to let the drug begin its magic. Her face relaxed and she felt like she was sitting in warm summer sun.

Mary opened the door to the toilet and Mrs. Reed was standing there with a security guard and the orderly.

"Ms. Breslin. Could you come with us please?"

Mary froze. Wide eyed, she looked at their stone serious faces. "What, I..." she was about to say something. An excuse. Anything. But instead she exhaled and was ushered into the vacated staff room.

"Please empty your pockets," Mrs. Reed demanded.

Mary shoved her hands into her pockets and fiddled with the evidence.

Mrs. Reed hovered over her like hawk about catch her prey. "Empty them. Now."

She emptied her pockets and put two cracked vials and three syringes on the table.

Frank burst through the revolving doors to the entrance of the hospital.

"Excuse me, Sir," a large security guard barked. "No one is allowed in at this time."

Frank stopped in his tracks. "I've come for my sister. Mary Breslin. She is a nurse here."

"Ha! Not anymore, she ain't." The guard stood with arms crossed, chest puffed out, with a smirk on his hairy face.

Frank's hands made a fist, then relaxed. "Where is she? Where is my sister?"

"She should be in jail. Or at the very least, detox. But she ain't." He pointed to a room at the end of the lobby. "Do you know what she did? She..."

Frank rushed past the guard and entered the dimly-lit room.

There, stooped in the corner, sat Mary. She looked up. Her cheeks were stained with tear-soaked mascara.

"Hey, little sister. Let's get you out of here. Get you home." Frank moved towards her with outstretched arms.

Mary stood up and fell into his chest. "Oh, Frankey. Thank you for coming. They took my keys away."

"It's okay. Let's just get out of here." He scooped up her belongings and got her to put her jacket on. He put his arm around her and escorted her past the scowling guard. He made no effort to help them.

"Goodbye and good riddance!" the guard said.

As they made their way out of the building, Frankey stopped, turned and stuck his middle finger up at the guard. The guard unfolded his arms and stuck his middle finger back at him.

They got into Frank's truck and left the parking lot.

Mary sat with her knees up to her chest and started to sob. "They caught me stealing a bit of morphine. For my dreadful back. It wasn't hurting anyone, I..."

"It's okay, Mary. We'll get this sorted out," Frank said.

"Oh, what will Mom and Dad think?" Mary shook her head. "It will be in the papers, I'm sure. And Mom is so ill again."

Frank turned onto the main road. "First things first. Ralph isn't staying with you anymore, is he?"

She glanced at him then turned away, "No. You know we're divorced now. He has his own place and no, he doesn't creep back to me. Like yours used to..."

"Okay, okay. That's all I needed to know." Frank blushed. "We'll go over to your place. Pick up a few things and then you can stay with me 'til we figure out what has to be done."

Mary put her hand out and squeezed his arm. "Thanks, Frankey. You're a rock."

The two sat in silence as the truck's headlights showed them the way forward in the middle of night.

Chapter 7

September 1988.

The overnight plane from Minneapolis landed into London Heathrow in the early morning. Numerous flights from all over the globe arrived at the same time creating an avalanche of people funneling into the passport and customs area. It excited Mary to see the mixture of races coming together. Sleepy eyed people from various parts of Asia, Africa, and Europe milled around the arrival area. It certainly wasn't Minneapolis. After a long wait, Mary finally made it through customs. As she came through the glass exit doors she scanned the people waiting for the incoming passengers. Placards with individual names held by tired drivers created a corridor for her and her fellow travelers to walk through. She looked past the posters searching for Michael's face. Though she had been to London before and knew her way around, he insisted on picking her up and driving her in. She caught sight of a man waving his arms up and down. It was Andrew, Michael's partner.

"Mary! Over here!" A big, burly, ginger-haired man stood grinning with his arms open wide. Two drivers parted, allowing Mary to pass between them with her luggage.

Andrew moved towards her, oblivious to the crowd around him. "Ach, Mary, how lovely to see ya!" His thick, Glaswegian accent was like warm syrup. She let go of her luggage and his massive arms wrapped around her thin body. His beard tickled her forehead. The people close to them jostled with each other creating more space for the two. He released her and beamed at her with his Cheshire cat grin. The smile then parted from his face. "Michael couldn't make it this morning. He had a wee accident."

Mary pulled back from him. "Oh no. Is he all right?"

"Oh he's fine," he assured her, "just a wee break in the ankle; they put him in a cast up to his knee."

Mary's brow furrowed. "God. When did this happen?"

"Last night. You were probably on the plane already." Andrew's arms waved in the air like two jellied eels. The nearby crowd gave him even more space to gesticulate. He remained unaware of their presence. He was totally focused on her. "It was the final rehearsal before the performance. The lead male in the piece just wasn't getting his steps, twists and turns correct." Andrew began to turn in an exaggerated pirouette. "And so Michael, in a rage, rushed onstage to show him the correct sequence and got tangled up. He fell and broke his leg!" The people around them turned and stared at Andrew's extravagant display. "So here I am!" The grin returned. "Let me take your bags, I remember you've a bad back."

"That's kind of you but..."

Andrew had already grabbed the luggage and was striding his way to the exit. To the crowd he was like Moses and like the sea, they parted. Mary rushed behind him in his wake. They took one of the black cabs that were lined up, like working ants, into the city.

Michael and Andrew had recently moved into a small, terraced house in North London. Andrew inherited money from his parents, allowing them to purchase a two-bedroom home with a walled garden. The combined income of a choreographer/dance teacher and an art critic didn't amount to much. They never would have been able to buy in this part of London without help. When Mary visited last time, they lived a one-bedroom apartment. She slept on the living room sofa with the two cats.

Andrew marched into the living room with Mary following him. "Here's the invalid."

Michael was sitting upright on a bright red sofa with a thin, grey blanket over him.

A shiny white cast surrounded his lower right leg. A single large, red heart was drawn on it.

He put his arms out. "Sister, welcome!"

Mary rushed over to him and they hugged. "Oh, Mikey."

Andrew stood back and beamed. "He's such a drama queen, your Michael. Tea, anyone?"

"Yes, that would be nice," Michael said. "Remember, Mary. They drink an awful lot of the stuff over here."

Mary perched herself on the edge of the sofa next to Michael. "I do." She said then called out to Andrew, "No sugar in mine please."

Andrew pointed a finger in the air as he walked away. "I remember. Two teas coming up."

Michael smiled at Mary. "Sorry about this." He pointed to the cast. "I'm really touched, you made the effort to come over. This is the first time I'm showing something at a big venue in London. It's called Sadler's Wells. It's not far from here."

"Oh, I'm so excited for you, Mikey. We all are." She looked down at her feet. "I so wish Mom could have come to see it."

Michael rubbed his face. "How is she?"

Mary put her arm on his shoulder. "Not good. The cancer has come back with a vengeance. Being Mom, she's trying to put a brave face on. But I can see through it. We're just trying to keep her comfortable."

"God, that's awful. She's lucky to have you there." He winked at her.

"Super nurse."

"Disbarred super nurse," Mary mused.

Michael took her hand. "How's that going?"

"One day at a time, as the rehab group says. In time, I plan to make fresh start of things in Florida. I can rehab there and then reapply for my license," Mary said. "Anyways that is why I'm over for just a few days. Got to get back to my rehab and Mom."

Andrew came strolling in with a silver platter. "Here we are! Tea and biscuits at eleven in the morning. Never too early."

Mary yawned. "Well it'd be five in the morning back home."

Andrew waved his finger at her. "No, no. The latest research shows one must set one's watch to the local time and think you're here. It's the best way to stave off jet lag." He poured the tea and gave each a cup. "So, Nurse Mary. Will he survive?"

Mary shook her head. "Umm… not sure."

"Do you know what I think?" Andrew arched his eyebrow.

Michael adjusted himself. "Mary, I don't think we have a choice."

Andrew pursed his lips. "I think he did it on purpose."

Michael laughed, threw his hands up, almost spilling his tea. "What?"

Mary and Michael were transfixed as Andrew strolled around the room with his cup of tea. "It's obvious. He is hoping for some sympathy from us vicious critics tomorrow night. He thinks we'll be easy on him because he has a little broken leg." He stops and stares at Michael. "But we see right through your desperate act."

Michael guffawed and turned to Mary. "See what I have to put up with around here?"

Mary grinned. "You two are quite an act."

"And. And..." Andrew said pitifully, "no one can tell you to 'break a leg' tomorrow night."

When they arrived at the venue, people were starting to gather. Michael was disappointed that it wasn't a sellout, but Andrew consoled him that no emerging choreographer could expect a full house. Especially the size of Sadler's Wells. Mary was encouraged to see most of the ground floor was full and most of the balcony had people looking down upon the stage. Originally, they were to sit in the middle of the audience a third of the way back. Now because of Michael's cast they sat on the side, in one of the boxes. Andrew gleamed. "Ach, we're just like fucking royalty! Where's the bloody champagne?"

Michael put his finger to his lips, "Shh..." he said with an embarrassed hush.

Andrew went to the front of the box and looked out onto the crowd in a regal manner. He turned to Mary. "A good turnout of my subjects, wouldn't you say?" Mary giggled.

"Andrew. Will you come and sit down please," Michael commanded.

Andrew took one more look at swarm of people below him. "Yes your highness. Immediately." He sat down next to Mary.

The music began to play, the lights dimmed, the audience hushed. A silence. Then curtain rose. A spotlight beamed on a still, solo figure with his back to the audience. A violin created a gentle, melodic tone and the dancer, still with his back presenting, moved almost imperceptibly to it. Mary intently watched and grabbed Michael's hand. They squeezed simultaneously and kept the grip. The lights rose on the stage and six other stationary dancers appeared. A quintet of strings thickened the sound and individually the dancers, one by one, began to move 'till all of them began to twist, turn, and glide amongst each other. A magic had descended upon the auditorium. The audience was spellbound. The changes of mood, color and tempo wove throughout the piece like three vibrant threads and kept it dynamic and alive.

The dance finished in the quiet manner in which it began. The spotlight dimmed, then went out. There was a moment of black stillness. Michael, Mary, and Andrew held their breath. The lights came back on to a roar of applause.

The troupe received a standing ovation and after the dancers took their bows, Michael was brought out on stage. The crowd shouted and clapped in approval as he gingerly came out on his crutches. Andrew stood next to Mary and loudly wolf whistled as he was presented with a large bouquet of flowers. Michael gushed and gestured to the audience as he awkwardly tried to hold the flowers. A dancer next to him saw his predicament, took them, and raised them to the audience. After a third recall, the curtain dropped. The audience took a collective breath of contentment, gathered their belongings and started to leave.

Andrew turned to Mary and gave her a crushing hug. "You must be so proud. WE must be so proud!" Mary nodded in agreement. They hurried out of the box to reunite with Michael.

A post-performance party was held backstage. Michael was swarmed by admirers, but he tried to include Mary as much as he could. After a bit, Andrew pulled her to the side.

"Let's let him bask in the adoration on his own. It's his night."

"Oh, yes please," Mary said, "I could kill for a cigarette."

"Yeah, let's. I'll grab another drink. You want..." Andrew abruptly stopped in mid-sentence. "Sorry."

"Don't apologize," Mary waved her hand dismissively, "it's my problem. Go get your drink and let's nip outside."

"A splendid plan!" Andrew spun and headed towards the bar.

Afterwards, a black cab hurdled the three through the empty streets of late-night London. Michael and Andrew surreptitiously stroked each other while the driver detected Andrew's accent and engaged him in Celtic versus Rangers football talk. The cabbie gagged with laughter when Andrew said he supported both teams. The driver explained to Mary that the teams were arch rivals and hated each other. Mary sat quietly and drank it all in.

The taxi pulled up to their house. They noisily got out of the cab. Michael's crutches kept him upright as he swayed in a drunken stupor. Andrew heavily tipped the driver. Mary took the keys off Andrew as he was fumbling with them and she opened the door. They piled in behind her laughing and directed her to the sofa where they all flopped into a giggling heap.

"Tea?" Mary shrilled in her best Julie Andrew's voice. "Cup of tea for the gentlemen?"

"Fuck tea," Andrew slurred. "A wee dram is what we need."

As they lay on the sofa, they became aware of a persistent beeping in the hallway. It was coming from their answer machine.

"Well I'm certainly not getting up to listen to it," Andrew said. "Probably another adoring fan for you, Michael. Telling you how marvelous you were. Are. I'm mean... either way, I'm not moving. Except to get the whisky." He got up and lunged towards the drinks' cabinet.

Mary looked at her brother. "You're in no state to stand up. Want me to listen and write down a message?"

Michael's eyes were closed. "Sure."

Mary got up and went into the hallway. Andrew had got the whisky and sat down on the sofa. Michael and him clinked glasses and chatted.

"Shhhhh!" Mary said from around the corner.

The machine was blinking showing that there was one message to be heard. Mary pushed the recall button. There was a pause; the line was crackling. "Mikey? Mikey? This is Frankey." Mary held her breath. She hovered over the machine. Michael's head jerked towards the machine. He handed Andrew his drink and stood up. "I'm calling from the hospital. I'm here with Dad and Anne."

"Stop!" Michael shouted and made his way to the hallway and leaned against the wall.

Mary turned off the machine until he was settled. He nodded and she turned the message back on. "I have some bad news. It's Mom. It's real bad..." Mary put her hand to her mouth and turned to Michael. "This is the number at the unit in the hospital 422-1784." They could hear Frank starting to cry. He cleared his throat. "That's 422-1784. I don't know how you dial international. Area code here 612. Is Mary with you? I, I don't know what more to say. Oh God... It's five in the afternoon here, makes it eleven at night there, I think. Call as soon as you can. Love you." The line went silent.

Michael went over the phone. They held each other as they listened to the message again. Andrew brought in Michael's whisky then returned to the living room. Michael dialed the number and they both listened to the faint ringing of the phone in the hospital. A nurse answered and they heard her call out for Frank.

Frank came to the phone. "Mikey. I'm afraid I have some bad news."

"Frankey. Mary is here with me. We are both listening," Michael said.

Frank's voice started to break. "Mom's died. She had a massive stroke."

There was silence on the line but for Frank breathing heavily.

"Where was she?" Mary asked.

"Dad found her in the kitchen. She..." Frank started to cry.

Michael and Mary could hear him sobbing. There was a rustling on the other end.

"Mary, Mikey? It's Anne." She had been standing next to Frank. "Hi. Yes, Dad found her in the kitchen when he got home from work." Her voice was cracking as well, but she carried on. "Dad had spoken to her at midday, she seemed fine."

"Did they try to resuscitate her?" Mary gripped the phone.

"The ambulance people did what they could but she was already dead when they got there," Anne said.

"Oh Jesus," Michael said. "How's Dad?"

"Hard to say," Anne sighed. "I think he's in a state of shock. Very quiet. They let us bring the dog in as he was with Mom when Dad found her. Dad just keeps stroking the dog."

"Take care of Dad," Mary said.

"I will. We can wait till you guys come back to start the funeral arrangements."

Michael took a sip of whisky. Mary grabbed the glass from him and drank the rest.

"Michael broke his leg yesterday," Mary said. "He is in a cast, he can't fly. I'll try to rearrange my flight and come back tomorrow or the next day."

"Oh, Mikey, sorry to hear. We'll miss you." Anne cleared her throat. "If you'd like us to say something at the funeral from you, we'll do it."

"Thanks. I will," Michael said.

The siblings all said goodbye to each other and the phone call ended. Mary and Michael held each other for a long time. Then they made their way back to the living room where Andrew was sitting with the two cats.

"I think we all could use a wee dram more of that whisky," Mary said.

Andrew sprung to his feet and the startled cats jumped off the sofa. "Coming right up."

Chapter 8

Frank crept in amongst the white birch trees and green pine. The wind had shifted in the hour he had been walking and now it was coming from the north east. It was a good wind direction. Frank calculated that for most of the hunt today he would be downwind of his prey. He stopped behind a pine tree and pulled out two arrows and examined their tips. They were both razor sharp. The men had used rifles for the first six years of hunting deer at the lodge. Last year he had brought his father to the lodge and had him sit in a stand with his rifle, while he tried to move deer towards him to no avail. So, Peter went back to hunt with his brothers, and this season Frank was determined to hunt with bow and arrow. This, he told the men, was true hunting; to wait, stalk, and then to get close enough to kill the deer with an arrow. Some of them protested and said that next he'd want them all to hunt in bearskins and feathers in their hair. But Frank persisted and, in the end, they all agreed.

He walked into the trees. He held a crouched position as he scanned the woods. He listened for any small movement. This continued for the next three hours; stopping, touching, listening, smelling, looking. He hadn't seen anything except for two fat grouse and a few day-old deer prints. His body was tired. Last night's escapades had come back. The cold was attacking him on all sides. His toes, fingers, and face were all beginning to ache. He stopped next to a large pine tree and under its low branches he found a spot clear of snow. Frank laid down his bow and arrows then sat with his back to the base of the tree. From the inside of his coat, he pulled out a small silver thermos and poured a cup of coffee laced with brandy. A rush of steam rose from the container and onto his face. The small icicles that had formed on his eyebrows and nasal hairs began to melt causing droplets of water to run down his face. He tasted his brandied coffee and felt its heat warm his belly.

His thoughts drifted back to the lodge. The other men would have risen from their beds by now. A couple of them might have ventured out for an hour or two but he knew that after a big breakfast most of them would say, "Ah, what the hell!" The cards would come out and they'd start to drink again. The second cup of coffee was starting to reach his cold toes. He loved the silence and the solitude of the forest. He felt part of it; he respected nature. Frank covered the thermos and put it back into his coat. He looked into the woods. His breathing slowed and his body relaxed against the tree. Even though he had just drunk coffee, a wave of tiredness swept over him. His eyelids began to flutter and then they closed.

Dark clouds gathered in the high hills north of the forest. The wind picked up pushing the clouds, and snow began to fall. Over the next hour, soft flakes fell onto the open ground and branches of the pines.

Frank woke and opened his eyes. He was covered in a thin veil of snow. He moved his hands and toes. They were stiff and tender, but mobile. He got up and reached for his bow then moved out from under the tree. It was then that he saw them. Fresh deer prints. They had not been there before. He was sure of that. The deer must have walked right by him when he was asleep and covered by the snow. Frank looked out into the forest then knelt down to study the hoof marks. Three or maybe four deer were moving along the ridge. He studied the prints again. One set was much larger than the others. *It could be the big buck.* Frank hooked the string of his bow and pulled an arrow out of the quiver. Attaching it to the string, he set off after the deer.

For the next hour, Frank followed the tracks. He paused, knelt down and took a close look at them. He took his glove off and touched them. He knew the deer were nearby.

Frank had seen the big buck in the autumn when he was duck hunting. It stood strong and erect on the edge of the swamp with its powerful shoulders and neck holding a huge rack of antlers. The buck looked out over the land. It had two does alongside him. Frank put his rifle down as he sat in the duck blind and admired the beast. The buck was the king of this land. Finally the buck turned and disappeared back into the forest with the does following him.

Frank continued his hunt through the forest in search of the deer.

Chapter 9

Mary and Michael's car followed the priest's black limousine as it headed north up the flat two-lane highway. In the back seat, their father sat with Frank's golden retriever. In one of his winter coat pockets, Peter had a photo of Frank and himself at the hunting lodge. They were dressed in matching camouflage hunting jackets and holding their rifles. They proudly stood before an orderly line of dead ducks at their feet. This was one of the last times the two had hunted together. It was a crisp, autumn day and they hid in a duck blind. They shot at the unsuspecting ducks as they flew overhead. The dead birds fell from the sky and hit the pond with a splash. Frank's retriever dog panted as he swam out to collect them. It was the perfect day for a father and son who hunted. In his other coat pocket, Peter had a small, red Indian doll that he found on his doorstep that morning.

"Warm enough for you, Dad?" Mary asked as she looked through her rear-view mirror.

Peter mumbled something as he stared out of the window at the passing frozen landscape. The dog's head rested on his lap.

Michael turned in his seat and glanced at him. "Dad, you okay?"

"I said I'm fine."

Mary and Michael exchanged glances then both looked ahead at the black flat road. Forests of scrub pine heavy with snow lined the road. Every few miles a weather-beaten barn and house broke up the desolate snowy landscape. Lights flickered from these isolated homes.

"That Father Benedict is nice guy. But nah, I don't buy it," Michael said.

"What's that?" Mary asked.

"The Catholic Church, God, the whole thing."

"Really? The whole thing?" Mary shifted in her seat.

Michael looked out the window and shook his head. "I was suspicious right from the start."

Mary smiled as she looked in the rear-view mirror. "Oh, here we go, Dad!"

"Yeah, right from the beginning. First communion. Remember first communion, sis?"

"Everyone remembers their first communion," Mary said.

Michael's hands rose into the air. "The host. The body of Christ. I went up to the altar. I was practically floating. I was going to receive 'The body of Christ'!"

"And?" Mary gave him a brief look.

"Oh man. I stick my tongue out. Close my eyes. I'm ready. BRING IT ON, I say. My soul IS ready!"

"AND?"

"And it was the most bland, dry, sticky thing I'd ever tasted in my whole life. It stuck to the roof of my mouth. I started to gag."

Mary began to giggle.

"Yeah, gag. Thought I was going to throw up. Right there in the pew. I tried to peel it off by using my tongue. I was trying to be subtle. I wanted to stick my finger and pull it off. Throw it on the floor. I looked around. Everyone else had their eyes closed, smiling, praying to their Lord."

"Oh, Mikey!" Mary guffawed.

"Yeah. So right then and there I thought 'is this it? Is this

what I am to believe in, adore? This nauseating cracker?'"
Michael shook his head and pointed. "Now if it tasted like an
Oreo cookie, he might have had a chance."

"Oh, Mikey…"

The car slowed and stopped at a stoplight. It was the only
intersecting road that they had come across in more than an hour.
Large trucks thundered down this road to the east. They were
taking their loads of long cut logs to the port of Duluth.

The signals changed and the funeral group continued its
journey north.

"You know." Mary opened her window and lit a cigarette,
blowing its smoke at the opening. "That was a nice speech you
gave, Mikey. A lot of people were in tears."

Michael looked at her, then at his hands. His voice cracked
a little. "I just wanted to say something about how we grew up as
brothers. I hoped the football story would do that."

"Yes, you guys never stopped playing. Whether it was
football, baseball or basketball," Mary said. "Sometimes you
would enlist us and the neighbors to play in your games.
Remember when Frankey accidentally hit that kid from across
the street with a basketball? Broke his glasses and nose. Blood
everywhere."

"Yeah, what was his name? Alan?" Michael asked.

"Alan Kholaski," Peter said.

"Yes, that's it," Mary said. "Dad, didn't you have to pay
damages?"

"Sure did. Bunch of dumb Polacks." He stroked the dog's
head. "Can I have one of those cigarettes?"

Michael took the pack out of Mary's purse. He lit two,
handing one back to his father. The other he kept for himself.

Mary looked over at him. "Since when?"

"Now," Michael said. He coughed and blew smoke out the window.

"What was that in the speech about Frankey protecting you?" Mary asked.

"Oh, it was nothing," Michael said.

Mary slapped him on the knee. "What was it?"

"Well, in tenth grade I had decided to stop all sports and concentrate on dance."

Peter interrupted. "You were a good basketball player. You could have made the varsity team in your sophomore year."

"I doubt that, Dad." Michael took a long drag from his cigarette and coughed again. "Anyway, it was the evening, and I had just come out from my dance rehearsal at the school. There were two guys out on the street, smoking. I think they were seniors, like Frank. They came over to me, and one of them said, 'Hey, we hear you're a fag. Wearing tights and prancing around. Is that right?' I said I just liked dancing. That's all. But that didn't satisfy them and they said they didn't like queers in this town. They grabbed me and told me they were going to teach me a lesson. There was no one around and they were big and strong. They dragged me around the corner of the school. They started to kick and punch me. I tried to tell them to stop and then just curled up to protect myself. But they were vicious and I had no choice but just take their beating. Then I heard this roar and I looked up and there was Frankey. He jumped on one of them and threw him off me, punching and kicking him like a mad man. The other guy left me and tried to help out his friend, but Frankey swatted him off like a fly. Within minutes both of them were scurrying down the street with Frankey chasing after them."

"I remember you coming home one night with Frankey. You were all beat up," Mary said. "Dad, did you call the police?"

"No." He blew out cigarette smoke. "We didn't want to involve them."

"We?" Michael threw his cigarette out the window. "Maybe you were afraid it would get out that I was queer."

Mary cut in. "Well, you were lucky Frankey happened to be there."

"Frankey was always there for me," Michael said.

"You should have continued to play basketball," Peter muttered. "Can we pull over at the next rest spot? I got to take a piss."

After a few miles a rest stop appeared. They pulled into it and the other cars followed. The priest's car waited by the side of the road. Once he was finished, Peter told Mary he'd ride the rest of the way to the cemetery in Anne's car. The cars pulled out of the rest station and got behind the priest's car once again. The dog spread out over the whole backseat of Mary's car. Peter had left the Indian doll for him to chew on. After a time, the dog fell asleep.

Chapter 10

Frank was nine and Michael was eight. In the spring, as soon as snow melted, they played baseball after school with a whiffle ball. A white, plastic baseball with slits. These holes reduced the speed of the ball when pitched, and its distance when hit by a bat. They played in the 'near backyard', the one closest to the house. It was surrounded by a white picket fence that created the sense of a ballpark. The 'far backyard' was an acre of open grassland that the family rarely used but still needed to be mowed by the boys once a fortnight during the summer months. Their game consisted of batting against each other. Frank was always the Minnesota Twins, and he cut the morning batting line-up out of the morning paper after the previous night's game. Michael was whichever team he wanted to be. He always scanned the line-ups looking for a team with a high proportion of right-handed batters, because, as they went through the line-ups, they had to bat the way the real batters did.

Michael was right-handed. Frank had a huge advantage, for not only was he a year older and a naturally gifted athlete, he was ambidextrous and very difficult to get out. They had modified the game over time. Two strikes including foul balls and that batter was out. Three balls a walk. Hitting certain distances gave the batter a single, double or triple, or a home run if it went over the white picket fence. There was no running involved. They played a full nine innings. The game took thirty to forty minutes to play, unless they were tied and went into extra innings.

"Okay, Mikey. Batter up!" Frank said, pounding the ball into his leather mitt.

"Who're you today?"

"The Cleveland Indians."

"Shit, they are dead meat." Frank's eyes focused at the imaginary catcher behind the plate for a sign as to which pitch to throw.

Michael did his customary digging into the batter's box. They were both obsessed with baseball but Michael was much more into the fine detail of the game. He knew all the idiosyncrasies of all the batters in the major leagues; how they gripped their bats, moved into the batter's box, made the sign of the cross or looked to the heavens for guidance before the first pitch. Cleveland's leadoff hitter was a particularly twitchy Puerto Rican; a neck-jerking, shoulder-rolling, gum-chewing bag of nervous-ness.

"Oh for Christ's sake. Get on with it!" Frank tried to act serious, but he couldn't contain a tiny smile as he watched his little brother's gesticulator antics before he settled in for the first pitch. Frank reared back and sent in a sizzling fastball, which Michael could only foul off. Strike one. And then they were off. Nothing could disturb them from the deeply woven fantasy that they devised. Michael even provided commentary between innings. He recited beer commercials, facts on the batters coming up, and the pitchers warming up in the bullpen. Frank mostly kept quiet. He only spoke to argue whether the whiffle ball was fair or foul, or whether the pitch was a ball or a strike. His intention was to win. And he nearly always did. For Michael, it was a chance to play with his brother and improvise. He created a world within the baseball game. The two produced a timeless bubble that was completely their own.

Chapter 11

The wooden boat slipped out onto the still lake in the early morning. His dad sat in the back, steering it from the handle of an outboard motor. Michael, ten years old, was huddled in the front. He was wrapped in a bright red jacket. He peered through his sleepy eyes, as the front of the boat cut effortlessly through the glass-like water. A thick mist still clung to the trees like cotton candy, waiting for the sun to burn it off. Michael shivered from the cold air. His father lit a cigarette, tilted his head back and blew a cloud of smoke into the sky. The boat continued across the lake over to the edge of a reed bed. Once it got there it slowed and they got ready to fish. His father leaned forward and put his hand into the bucket of bait. A silver minnow was grabbed and deftly hooked through its lips. The bait was put in the water, and the lead weights on the fishing line dropped it to the bottom of the lake. Upon feeling the minnow hit the floor, his father jerked up on the tip of his fishing rod, then reeled in a bit of line so the bait could move just along the floor.

Michael watched his father's agile movements. He tried to mimic them and gingerly put his hand into the ice-cold bucket of water and grabbed a minnow. It squirmed and wriggled in his small hand. Michael's tongue poked out of his mouth, urging his fingers to use just the right amount of pressure to control and hook the minnow without squashing it.

His father took his eyes off the lake and studied his son's feeble efforts. He sighed. "Get that minnow into the water before it dies."

Michael's hands tensed as he continued to fumble with the wet, greasy bait.

"Jesus…" he heard his father mutter.

Finally, the metal hook pierced the minnow's lips. He threw it into the water and let out some line. He glanced at his father and exhaled a sigh of relief.

They were the only fisherman on the lake. The surrounding forest absorbed the low purring sound of the motor. Michael shivered and tried to keep warm by sinking deeper into his coat. His father didn't seem to notice the chill. The motor suddenly sputtered and stopped, causing the boat to veer towards the shoreline. His father scowled through his cigarette smoke. He violently pulled on the motor's cord and the engine stuttered, popped loudly, and died. He stood up in a crouched position to gain more leverage. He jerked the cord again and again. "You son of a bitch. Start!"

Startled ducks at the water's edge flapped their wings and swam into the reeds for shelter. Finally, the motor responded with a roaring sound. His father put the motor into reverse and moved out of the weed bed. The boat repositioned and continued to troll down the lake.

His father loved to wake early and be on the lake. His mother and his two sisters lay in bed most of the morning. When they woke, they read glossy magazines while the men fished. Frank couldn't join the family as he was playing in a baseball tournament all week. When Frank was around, Michael didn't have to accompany his father on these fishing trips. Michael wished he was snuggling up with his sisters in their warm bed, laughing with them at the pop stars in the magazines.

This was his father's week away from the monotonous grind

of his work. A week of relaxation; the peace of the lake, the fishing, and fresh air. His father wanted Michael to appreciate it too. Every morning on this vacation he took him out onto the lake to teach him to fish. This is what men did with their sons.

The crimson fishing line suddenly snapped tight across the still water. The force from within the lake practically pulled the fishing rod from Michael's sleeping hands.

"No, no. Leave my hook alone," he muttered to himself. The line went limp and it coiled lazily on the surface. He was relieved that it had let go. They continued to move down the lake. The line became taut again, leaving the minnow to dance along the bottom. This would tempt the fish lurking in the fallen trees and thick weed beds.

These trees and weeds were what Michael always caught. The heavy logs would snap his line and cause his father to curse. "Why can't you feel it's a branch and pull it away? Why do you have to break the God damn line all the time?" His father and Frank rarely got their line caught. They would just have a quick flick of the wrist and the hook would be free. Yesterday Michael pulled in a large clump of weeds. His father was poised with the landing net, only to see weeds emerge from the lake rather than a fish. He scowled at his son and threw the net on the bottom of the boat. Its vibrations had sent a shiver through Michael that had lasted most of the day and had given him nightmares last night.

The line began to pull again. Michael looked at his father. He hoped that his father hadn't seen the movement of the rod. Cigarette smoke obscured his father's face, except for his sharp black eyes looking forward and watching the shoreline. His father hadn't noticed. The boat continued to slip in and out of the small bays, keeping to the edge of the murky weed bed.

Michael thought about his sisters again. They would be

huddled together in their bed with a heavy chequered quilt over them, drinking hot chocolate while reading 'Bright Stars' and 'Show Bizz Weekly'. Two days ago, in the afternoon, while their father was sleeping, all three of them dressed up in skirts and blouses and raced out into the woods pretending to be abandoned by their parents and being followed by a bear. Michael loved the feeling of air rushing up between his legs as he ran screaming through the pine trees. When they ran out of breath, they fell onto the pine needle floor into a heap of uncontrollable laughter. They grabbed each other and tickled till they nearly wet themselves. When they returned to the cabin, their mother saw them and she put a finger to her lips. They valiantly tried to stifle their laughter, as they changed into their normal clothes and cleaned the makeup off their faces. At supper, Michael noticed his father scrutinizing him. Had he left some eyeliner on? His father continued to look at him, but said nothing.

A fish grabbed his bait with its hidden hook and it lashed out to free itself. Michael's spine jerked to attention. The end of the rod was bent over with its tip touching the surface of the water.

"No, no, no," Michael said under his breath.

The fish heaved and twisted in the depths, trying to free itself.

Michael noticed that his father saw him struggling at the front of the boat. "What is it? What is it?" he said.

"I don't know."

"What ya mean, don't know?" His father glared at him. He then stood up and began to move towards him. The boat swayed from side to side. "Give the damn rod to me!"

Michael leaned forward to hand the pole to him but the pull from the lake was too strong. The rod would fall into the lake if he let go. He pulled it back into his body. His small hands gripped the handle of the rod and he leaned back. The force from the lake pulled against him. He began to reel in the line.

"Is it a fish?" his father asked. He stood in a crouched position, poised to move forward. He watched his son struggle with the rod.

Michael didn't answer. His eyes were fixed to where the line entered the lake. His hands ached from the force of the pull. His father moved to the back of the boat and sat down. He turned off the motor and the boat began to drift towards the middle of the lake. The sun had made its way over the tops of the trees and its sharp rays hit the side of the boat. The mist was beginning to thin, exposing the large green pine that surrounded the water. The two small figures sat alone in their boat, in the center of the lake.

His father could not restrain himself. "Keep the tip out of the water. Keep it up! Bring in the line!" He threw the lit cigarette into the lake. "Don't give him any slack right now or he'll go under a log and break the line."

Michael kept the reel close to his chest. His whole body was now fighting the fish. Slowly, the line came in. The sound of the steady buzz of the reel was all that he could hear. He wondered, *Is it a fish?* His father brought in his own line and then cautiously moved forward in the boat with the landing net. He saw his father looking at him and then at the water. The tip of the rod jerked back and forth as the fishing line danced across the water. The fish came to the top, its tail snapped the surface. They both saw it. It then plunged into the depths once again, the rod bent in two.

"Big fish! Give him some slack now, let him run a bit. Don't lose him!"

Michael stood up and let more line out. The boat rocked back and forth. His father lunged towards him but practically fell out of the boat.

"Give it to me! Give me the rod!"

His father stretched out his hand towards him. Michael looked at him and shook his head. He turned his attention back to the rod and reeled in the line. He kept the tip up above the water. He leaned back as far as he could and fought against the pull of the fish. He could feel it moving back and forth deep in the water trying to escape. The fight continued for a few minutes. Michael's young body began to tire from the battle. He gritted his teeth and grunted as he reeled in the fish. His father watched in silence. The fish finally came to the surface. Its black fin splashed in the water, its powerful curling tail waving in defiance. It dived again. Michael's spine tensed as he leaned back, fighting the pull of the fish. He could sense the line was about to snap. He let it out a little and began to reel it in again. He didn't dare look at his father who was hovering over him with a landing net in his hands. The fish continued to fight; diving, twisting, and trying to shake the metal hook from its jaw. Michael held firm.

The exhausted fish finally came to the surface. The water rippled but before the fish dove again his father deftly leaned over the side of the boat and scooped the fish out of the water. The boat nearly capsized due to the weight all on one side. His father quickly moved to the opposite side to steady it. The fish, in the net, slapped wildly in the air. A veil of water flew off the fish's scales and into Michael's face. He jerked away but was mesmerized by the fish. He could see its dark, menacing eyes looking at him while its powerful gills moved in and out, searching for water. It continued to flip and curl while his father grabbed it from underneath its gills and tore the hook from its jaw. He held it aloft admiring its size then beckoned to his son to come closer. Michael was scared. He did not want to be anywhere near the fish. He threw the rod down on the bottom of the boat and moved further away from both of them. The fish's green scales glistened in the sun and thick, red blood seeped from its torn jaw. Michael turned away from his father and the fish, and sat down at the end of the boat. He closed his eyes to try and prevent tears from rolling down his cheeks. His heart was pounding in his chest and he was having difficulty catching his breath. In his head screamed the words, *Big fish! Big fish!*

The next morning Michael hid under his bed when his father came in to wake him to go fishing. Michael could see his father's boots stop in front of the bed.

"Michael?"

The boots shuffled back and forth.

"Michael? Let's go fishing."

Michael held his breath. He heard his father sigh then leave the room. A few minutes later the motor on the boat started. Michael could hear it move away, out into the lake. He crawled out from under the bed, went to his sister's room and snuggled up with them.

Michael never fished with his father again.

Chapter 12

"Your cheating heart will tell on you..." Hank Williams sang on the radio.

Peter opened up the top of his shirt. He took off his tie and threw it on the car seat next to him. He put on his sunglasses and lit a cigarette. It was Friday evening. Work was done for the week and he had a three-hour drive up north, to the cabin where his family stayed for their summer vacation. He left work an hour early and drove through the monotonous suburbs before the rush hour traffic could build up. At the edge of the final suburb, he pulled into the parking lot of a liquor store. It was a dull, brown-brick building with a red and green neon sign flickering in the front window. He slid his car in between two pick-up trucks. In one of them a young, muscled man sat slumped in his seat with a baseball cap pulled over his eyes. He had 'SMOKEY' tattooed on his bulging bicep. Peter watched the man for a minute. He contemplated opening his door and taking the keys out of the ignition. Then he would give them to the store owner for safe keeping till the guy sobered up. Instead he just got out of the car and slammed the door sufficiently to startle and wake the man. Peter nodded at the ruffled figure and then entered the store with a wry smile of his face.

The stacks of bottles and cans of beer glimmered under the naked neon lighting. Muzak, with its sugary stringed violins, pierced the refrigerated air. He walked over to one of the humming refrigerators and pulled out a six pack of Colt 45, a strong malt liquor. The overweight man behind the counter took forever to get off his chair to serve him. He made no eye contact and didn't try to sell him anything else. He just took his money and sat down again.

"Missing you already, Buddy," Peter said as he left with a six pack under his arms. He stepped out of the cool shop and back into the hot, humid evening. The pick-up truck was gone but the man had left a bag of garbage on the hood of Peter's car. He cursed under his breath. He grabbed the bag and put it in a nearby trash can. A thick grease stain remained on the hood where the bag sat. Peter started the engine and reversed out of his space. He spun the car out onto the highway.

He could have taken a quicker route up north on the two lane, flat interstate but he preferred the one lane highway. The original. This one snaked its way through forested hills, lakes, and valleys while passing through small, sleepy towns. One of Peter's hands searched on the radio dial for a local station while the other steadied the car. He found a clear channel playing country western. His free hand then undid a can of beer and snapped the tab open. He checked his rear-view mirror for police. All clear. He then tipped the can up to his lips and let strong cold beer flow into his parched throat. He began to hum along with the music. The first can of beer slid down effortlessly. When he had finished it, he checked his rear-view mirror again, then flung the can out of his open window into the ditch. He opened another. His body began to relax from the demands of week.

Work bored him. He was a supervisor on various engineering projects in the city: buildings, roads, and bridges. He had done it for sixteen years. There was little challenge to it. The only stress was dealing with the workforce under him. But the pay was reasonable and he had a family to support. This would be his life

64

till retirement in twenty years. He threw the empty second can out the window and opened a third. His oasis from this routine life was the cabin by the lake.

His parents were German immigrants. They were industrious people and ran a hardware store in a northern town on the iron ore range. After school time, weekends, and summer holidays were spent behind the counter helping out in the store. His father had a small appliance repair shop in the back and it was there that he learned the rudiments of electricity and properties of metal and wood. When he was eighteen, World War Two began and he immediately enlisted. He used his skills and was a mechanic in the army. He kept the jeeps, tanks, and trucks in top working order as the American forces pushed into Europe to defeat the Axis Powers.

Peter covered up the remaining cans of beer on the seat next to him with his jacket and slowed down as he entered the little town of Cook. He once stopped here and bought a bag of pretzels. He went to the counter and playfully asked the shop owner, "What's cooking?" The owner just stared at him. After the only stoplight in town, Peter noticed two police cars sitting under a large oak. The cops sat on the hoods of their cars and lazily looked at him. He held his breath. He drove on and took quick glances in the rear-view mirror. Peter let out a sigh of relief as he left the city limits. He kept his speed down and continued to check his rear-view mirror for the next few miles. Satisfied, he pulled out another can and opened it.

When the war finished, he went to St. Cloud State and studied engineering. He was an older student, twenty-three, studying on the GI Bill. He hung around other returning soldiers. He embellished his wartime activity with a couple fictitious battles with the Nazis. He suspected most of them did this. It was the quiet ones whom he thought must have seen real battle. These men circulated in ones and twos. They rarely joined the larger, more boisterous ex-soldier groups.

The women at the university intimidated him. He had never come across women with such independent, bright minds. He shied away from their articulate discussions and confident manner. In his second year he met a young local woman in the drugstore. This was Sally. Her blond hair, pulled back in a ponytail, and her clear blue eyes, mesmerized him. She worked behind the counter, helping the pharmacist. After he'd met her, he kept going back every day. He bought aspirin one day, Band Aids the next.

"You must get injured a lot," she teased. She liked his shy but determined manner.

Finally, he plucked up the courage to ask her out.

"Well, if we do go out and have an accident, you have a very well stocked first-aid kit!" She smiled. "Sure," she said.

Soon they were meeting up most days. He had to put up with her playing in golf tournaments on the weekend. She was a good player and very keen. He would drive her to the surrounding golf clubs then go off to study or fish. Then he'd be there to take her home after she finished playing. He won over her parents by doing repairs around their house and taking her father fishing. After graduation, he was offered a job in Minneapolis. He asked her to marry him. She said yes, but was anxious that she would have to move away from her hometown. He told her they were both moving to a foreign place and this would be an adventure. They would create their own life. And St. Cloud was only an hour from the northern suburbs where they were going to live. She finally agreed. Within a year they were married. They bought a small house with garden in the suburbs. They had difficulty conceiving a child, but after three years, Frank was born. And the routine of adulthood began.

Peter finished his third can of beer as he entered Twin Pines. It was a small town on the edge of an Indian reservation. It was a town he knew well.

It was one year ago. The drive north had been difficult. He'd been driving for two hours through heavy thunderstorms with high winds. The driving required all his attention. He hadn't been drinking. The storm passed and the sun came back on this warm, July evening. His grip on the wheel started to relax when the engine in his car began to rattle and cough.

"Ah, Christ," he muttered. He knew immediately it was the carburetor and pulled over to the side of the road. He got out of his car. Pine trees lined the road and he could hear dogs barking in the distance. Peter opened the hood of his car and leaned over the engine. The smell of gasoline and oil was thick. His hands were quickly an oily black as he tried to free the stuck mechanism. He flipped the little metal flap back and forth several times, but it was clear it would not reset itself.

He stood back from the car. "Goddammit." He went to the trunk and pulled out a screwdriver and pliers from his toolbox. He fiddled further with the damaged device. After a few minutes of futile attempts, he hung his head and sighed. The crickets from the nearby woodland created a constant hum. He looked at the engine one more time then slammed the hood down. He kicked the front bumper. A small dent appeared from his frustration. He packed his tools away and got into the car. He started it and he was able to limp into Twin Pines. He drove into the only filling station in the town. It was a small white building with peeling paint and a faded red sign saying, 'Joe's Gas and Garage'. Peter stood in the vacant front of the shop and heard a radio at the back of the garage.

"Hello. Anyone there?"

There was a stirring in the back. Out of the shadows shuffled a tall, lanky Indian man in his mid-forties. About the same age as Peter.

"Hi. I've got some trouble with my car. Think it's the carburetor. Can you have a look at it?"

The man rubbed his hands on a soiled cloth. "Bit late in the day." He saw the disappointment on Peter's face and noticed his dirty hands. "But, sure. Bring her in and let's have a look."

Peter drove the car into the garage. The man opened the hood and hung a light on its inside latch. He bent forward and inspected the engine.

Peter stood next to him. "So, are you Joe, then?"

The Indian didn't look up. "Suppose I am. The real Joe died a few years ago. I worked with him. I bought the business off his wife. She moved to Arizona. I liked the name. The whole town did. So I kept it." With his screwdriver he tightened and tested the metal flap.

"Where ya headed?" Joe asked.

"Mantoba Lake."

The Indian stood up with the carburetor in his hand. The oil on it gleamed in the early evening light. "Not tonight, you ain't. Look here."

The men stood together inspecting the part. Joe pointed to the damaged piece with his screwdriver.

"Worn right through. You need a replacement. You'd probably last another ten miles before it blew completely."

Peter examined the damaged part, "Damn. Do ya have a replacement?"

"Nah, not in stock. I will call around this evening. Should be able to get you one by tomorrow morning. Be on your way by ten."

"Damn," Peter said again. Half his treasured time off this weekend would be spent in this sleepy little town. "Don't suppose there is place to stay around here?"

The man put the carburetor on the nearby bench. "Ray's Tavern up the road has food and lodgings. I can give you lift in a couple of minutes once I close up."

Peter studied him. The Indian's calm and friendly manner put him at ease. "Sure, Joe. If that wouldn't be too much trouble. Is there a pay phone around here? I have to speak to my wife."

Joe pointed to a door. "The washrooms in there. You can clean up then use my phone in the office while I close up."

Peter called Sally and then collected his belongings for the night. Joe's pick-up truck was out back and he got in. It was damp and smelled of fish, oil, and tobacco.

The engine of the pick-up belied the beat-up nature of the frame and started with one twist of the key. It purred with an assured, robust strength. Joe jerked the gear stick and let up on the clutch. They pulled out onto the main road. Peter looked out of the window at the porched, wooden houses set back from the road. Dirt driveways led to their front doors. Dogs lay on the steps to these porches, while children ran around on ill-kept front lawns.

"Live in the town, Joe?"

Joe was lighting a cigarette with one hand while steering with the other. He nodded to the pack on the dashboard and Peter took one and the lighter from him. Their smoke briefly intertwined then dashed out of the windows.

"Live on the reservation."

"Family, kids?"

"Had. But the wife moved away with them. She said I was too boring." Joe laughed to himself. "I probably am." He took another puff of his cigarette and blew it at the ceiling. "She is now living with some drunken chief on another reservation and I got me a boring wife." They both laughed.

"How 'bout you?"

"Four kids, wife. Live down in The Cities. I was born up on the Iron Range. We have a cabin up north. The family stays there for the summer. I go up there on the weekends. That's about it."

They pulled up in front of the tavern. Peter turned to him and said, "Hey, thanks a lot for the ride. Buy you a drink?"

Joe stared straight ahead. "I don't drink."

Peter shrugged.

Joe turned to him, "You know, there are lots of us Indians that don't drink. Boring, huh?" He turned the truck off. "But I'll have a Coke."

They got out of the truck and entered Ray's. Joe told Peter to sit at a table and he'd be back with a beer and a Coke in a minute.

"Let me pay for it," Peter said. But Joe had his back to him already and just waved his hand in acknowledgement.

The lights were dimmed in the tavern. Country and Western music rolled out of the lit juke box in the corner. The baseball game flickered on the television above the bar. A few heads turned from watching the game and nodded at Joe. Joe went up to the barman and they had a few words. The barman looked over at Peter and saluted him. Joe and the barman had a little joke. He then came back with a cold beer and a Coke.

"Ray says he can give you a room and a good steak meal for twenty dollars. For another five bucks he can provide some entertainment, too."

Joe winked at him. Peter looked him straight in the eye and then lifted his bottle and drank the beer. The cool alcohol was welcome and he finished it swiftly. He got up and fetched another before Joe began his Coke. Peter came back and sat down and leaned back on his chair.

"So, Joe. I noticed a couple of army photos in your office. Where did you serve?"

"Never got further than San Diego. I was a mechanic in the army. Worked on the tanks and jeeps for war against the Japs."

"Yeah, me too." Peter took a drink of his beer.

"Where? In the Pacific?"

"Nah. In Europe. England first. Then, after the landings, we followed the troops into France then Germany."

Joe sipped his Coke. "See any action?"

"Well, not really," Peter said. "I mean we occasionally saw trucks bringing back the dead and the wounded. Heard artillery fire in distance, bombing at night. But nah, nothing. Seeing all those wounded and dead soldiers made me feel lucky I had a skill. A mechanic." He took another swig of his beer.

Dolly Parton was singing her heart out from the jukebox. The smell of cooking meat was in the air.

"Yeah, me too," Joe said. "We were all prepared to go out and support the troops as they moved from island to island, but then they dropped the A bomb and that was it." Joe looked from side to side and then leaned closer to Peter. "But I got a couple of women into bed telling them that I was at Iwo Jima."

Peter rocked back on his chair, almost falling backwards. "Ha! Well, I was one of first to see the dead Hitler in his bunker! That, I can tell you, got me a lot of action too."

They talked a bit more about their mutual love of hunting

and fishing. The ones that were caught and killed and the ones that got away. Peter's steak came and Joe stood up to leave.

"That looks good," Joe said. "Enjoy your meal. See you in the morning. I'll drop by about nine and pick you up. I should have the carburetor by then and we can put it in together."

Peter stood up. "Sounds good to me." They shook hands. "What's your real name, Joe?"

"Ah, Joe will do."

"Well, Joe. Thanks again for helping me out."

Joe nodded and turned to leave. He shuffled out of the door in his scruffy cowboy boots. Peter turned his attention to the steak. It was huge and hung over the edges of the plate. His steak knife cut into the tender meat. The blood red juices oozed out.

After he finished his steak, Peter went up to the bar and sat down. He drank another beer and chased it with a shot of whisky. He watched the final innings of the ball game. He bought beers for two guys next to him, joked and traded fishing stories.

Peter was unsteady on his feet when he stood up to go to his bed for the night. Ray took his money for the meal, beers, and lodging. He ordered one of the waitresses to escort Peter to his room. Peter closely studied her backside as he followed her. It was a simple building outside and behind the tavern. There were five doors lined up under a dull streetlamp. The waitress opened the door and gave him a towel.

He held the towel and stared at her. "Would you like to stick around? Keep me company? I could get some drinks in," he said.

She said goodnight and hurriedly left.

Peter sat on the bed and looked at the closed door. There was a hot, solid bulge in his trousers. He lay back on the bed. His head was swirling but his groin and its needs overrode the strength of the alcohol. He stood up decided to go back to the bar. Joe had said something about 'extra'. He threw some water on his face

72

and looked at himself in the mirror. A thick day's stubble covered his face and a lock of his dark curly hair hung on his forehead like a solitary wave. He put his hand down the front of his trousers and adjusted his hard cock that pressed up against his zipper. Most times when he arrived at the cabin, his wife would be asleep. She would wake to greet him, then turn her back him and fall back to sleep. She couldn't satisfy him anymore. He was forty-three and still ravenous. She had become an obliging and dutiful wife. Her life was wrapped up in caring for their four children and running the household. Sex was not important to her anymore. She would respond sometimes if he wanted it. But she never initiated it anymore.

There was a knock on the door. Peter bolted upright and staggered over to the door. In the darkness stood a young Indian woman. Her eyes were cast down and her hands were clasped together.

"Hello," Peter said. "Who are you?"

She glanced up at him. "Mr. Ray thought you might like some company."

She was eighteen years old. She had long black hair tied in a braid. Her large brown eyes darted around him, avoiding eye contact. Peter could see her slim strong body under a blue floral dress.

"Come in." Peter moved back and opened the door fully.

She hesitated for a moment and then entered. He looked outside, to the left and right. There was no one around. He closed the door. She went over to the foot of the bed, then turned and looked at him. Peter was struck by her beauty. He turned on the bedside lamp and switched main light off. He hastily closed the curtains. Peter moved to her and took her hand. He pressed himself against her. Her body tensed. He ran his fingers through her dark hair and pressed his lips onto her soft, brown neck. Her body started to relax. She smelled of lavender and woodsmoke.

"You smell nice. What's your name?"

"Alice," she said.

Peter tried to control his lust. His hands ran down her delicate back and rested on her ass. He pressed their pelvises together.

"Hmmm... that's nice. You're lovely," he said.

She kept still, with her head tilted into his chest. She didn't make eye contact.

"How much?"

"Five dollars," she whispered.

His hands went under her dress and he caressed her ass. She stayed still, wooden. He got her to raise her arms, then lifted her dress over her head and let it drop to the floor. He guided her with care onto the bed. He hovered over her as she lay in her bra and panties. Alice looked at him nervously. Then she pulled back the sheets and got underneath them. She brought the sheets up to her neck.

"Don't worry, I'll be gentle," Peter said. He took off his shirt, trousers, and t-shirt. He left his undershorts on with his erect penis. Peter got under the sheets next to her. He felt her warm skin next to his. He kissed her face, neck and shoulders. Alice laid passively and let his kisses cover her. He moved to her soft belly. Peter was lost in her young body and could feel her beginning to respond to his caresses as her hips began to undulate. He helped her take off her underwear. Then he took his off. He hesitated as they lay in expectant nakedness. Then he kissed her all over again. Alice's body responded to him. He spread her legs and he eagerly entered her. The bed rocked back and forth noisily as he moved inside her. She gave out a muffled cry. Peter groaned in pleasure as he came. His body swiftly crumpled in an exhausted heap on top of her. They lay motionless for a minute. Their breathing fell into rhythm with each other. Scores of crickets hummed outside. Fireflies danced with each other. Alice maneuvered herself from beneath him. She went to the bathroom to clean herself while Peter turned over and lay on his back.

Large trucks rumbled by on the nearby road carrying newly cut logs to a sawmill. Peter hummed to himself.

The toilet flushed, the bathroom door opened and Alice tentatively came back into the room. She made no eye contact and hurriedly began to put on her underwear. Peter propped up on his elbows and looked her beautiful body. He couldn't let her go. He sat up fully, leaned over and grabbed her hand pulling her towards him. She tried to pull away but couldn't match his strength and reluctantly came toward him.

"It's okay Alice." He eased his grip on her. "I won't hurt you. I just want to be with you a little longer." His penis was erect again. "I'll pay you more."

Alice looked at him and his hard penis. She half smiled and took off her underwear.

"Okay."

She got back into bed and laid on her belly. She lifted her ass towards him. She turned her head towards him and nodded.

Peter immediately got behind her and gripped her buttocks. She pushed back towards him and he entered her. The bed rocked back and forth on its base. He moaned as he held onto her ass, rhythmically going in and out of her. After a couple minutes Peter gripped onto her hips and came even more deeply than the first time. Every part of his body felt the hot passion within. He gasped then fell onto the bed next to her and smiled with satisfaction. Peter had never experienced such deep organisms. And two of them! He took Alice into his arms. Alice lay with him for a few minutes. They didn't speak. His breathing and heart began to slow and his body relaxed. When his body became limp, Alice released herself from his grip. This time she wiped herself briskly and put on her clothes. Peter woke from his pleasant slumber. He got up and reached for his trousers and handed her a ten-dollar bill and two ones. She took them and turned to leave.

"Can I see you again when I'm passing?" he asked.

She looked up from the floor. "Ask Ray." She opened the door, then walked out into the night.

Peter looked both ways to see if anyone was around. He noticed she hadn't. "Good night," he called out as he watched her walk down the street. He closed the door, ambled to the bed and fell onto it in a satisfied heap. He was asleep as soon as his head touched the pillow.

Twin Pines became a regular stop for him over the next year. He never stayed over. He just stopped for a beer and an hour with Alice.

But tonight he would not stop. His cock had woken like clockwork as he had entered the town.

He looked at his groin. "Hey, stop it down there."

He was tempted as the heat built up in his trousers. They had friends coming to the cabin for the weekend. He promised Sally he'd get there by seven o'clock to help prepare for their visit.

Peter glanced down at his cock again. "Sorry, pal. You're not going to meet your friend Alice tonight. You're just going to have to settle down." He gave it a little rub. As he left the city limits, he checked his rear-view mirror. Not a car in sight. He opened another beer and turned the radio up.

Chapter 13

It was evening and a cool darkness was descending in the forest. Sally stood at the cabin door and shouted, "Come on, kids! It's time for bed! Finish up your game and come inside!"

She put the last of the dried dishes away and hung up the towel to dry. The children yelled and shrieked as they rushed past, followed by the barking dogs. They had just finished a raucous game of kick the can. Even their two dogs got involved. They barked loudly as Frank swept past an inattentive Mary and kicked the can, liberating his two siblings. Little Mary burst into tears. Sally had to go out into the yard earlier to console her. They were all in their bedrooms now putting their pajamas on, brushing their teeth, and getting into bed. This was the time Sally liked best at the cabin; the children in bed quietly reading or falling asleep and the dogs dozing. This was her time. She eagerly went to the refrigerator and got out a bottle of beer. She tiptoed through the living room so as not to disturb the children and sat down in the rocking chair on the screened-in porch.

She gazed out onto a still lake surrounded by pine and birch trees. Two loons swam in the middle of the lake, diving for fish. When they resurfaced, they screeched their eerie prehistoric sound. The light on the porch attracted large bugs and moths. Sally rocked in the chair and watched them smash against the screen as they hurtled towards the light. She finished her beer and got up to check on the children. The boys were reading in their double bed with Sammy, their golden retriever, asleep at the foot of the bed.

"Ten more minutes, boys. Then lights out."

Michael sat up in bed. "Oh, Mom!"

"Not another word." Sally crossed her arms. "Or it will be lights out now."

The boys looked at her and shrugged their shoulders in defeat.

She went into the other room to check on the girls. The light was already out, and girls were asleep with Jackie, their old, brown cocker spaniel, lying between them. Sally got another beer and returned to the porch. She turned on the radio low to listen to her favorite program, the baseball game. When she was growing up in St. Cloud, her mother used to listen to the games when she was cooking or knitting in the evening. Her father or husband were never particularly interested and it was Sally who passed on the obsession of baseball to her children. Occasionally, if one of her children were restless, she'd let them sit with her while she knitted and listened to the game. But they had to be quiet or she would order them back to bed. Tonight, the Twins had an important game against Detroit, and she was glad the children were all settled. The light in the boys' room went out.

Sally and Peter bought the cabin two years ago. They decided it would be better for her and the children to spend their summers up on a lake rather than in the suburbs. The children's ages ranged between Frank at eleven and Mary at six. When it wasn't raining, Sally made sure that the children were outside most of the day, only coming in for meals. She watched the boys play baseball, the girls build forts, and all of them swim and fish. It was a different kind of education for them. They all looked healthy and happy here.

Having the children and then raising them had taken a lot out of Sally. She tired easily, even though she was only forty. Being at the cabin allowed her to structure her day so that she did all the domestic tasks but still had time to rest. She liked the time she had to herself at the cabin. Peter had two weeks' vacation a year from his work. He spent one of them deer hunting and the other with them at the cabin. That was fine with Sally. She found that she really didn't miss him. After dealing with the demands of the children all day, she didn't particularly want to talk to or be with anyone else. So the ballgame and a beer was the perfect way to end the day. Especially if the Twins won.

Childbirth had been had been very traumatic for Sally. Every birth had required cutting and many stitches. She found that Peter was not very understanding to her situation and he was very eager to resume sex as soon as possible after every birth. She once tried to explain to him that it simply hurt.

He just stared at her and shook his head. "I'm a man."

When Friday evening came, Sally would forgo the baseball game and make sure that she was in bed and pretending to be asleep. She would hear the car coming down the dirt drive and see the headlights dance on trees. She closed her eyes and inched to the edge of the bed. She pulled down her nightdress and turned her back to the middle of the bed. Peter would come into the bedroom, take off his clothes, and lay down next to her.

"Sally? You awake?"

"Hi Honey," she'd say in sleepy tone. She kept her back to him.

Peter moved in closer. He could feel her body stiffen. "Sally?" There would be a period of cold silence. She finally heard him grunt and turn his back to her, tugging at the blankets. The smell of beer, lavender and woodsmoke permeated the room.

But tonight was not a Friday night. It was Wednesday and Sally was in her chair, with her beer. The Twins were ahead 4-1 in the top of the eighth. If they won, they would go into first place. Sally rocked in her chair in a slow peaceful rhythm. Tonight, life was good.

Chapter 14

August 1981. Ten years earlier.

"What do you mean, you're moving to England?" Frank said. He looked at Michael as he took a sip from his beer.

They were sitting on the third base side, ten rows back from the dugout. The best seats in the house. Or at least they thought so.

"I've had a great offer from a dance company there," Michael's black Converse shoes crunched on the peanut shells that lay at his feet.

"Do Mom and Dad know?"

The crack of the bat drew their attention back to the field. The baseball flew between the center and right fielders.

"Go for two!" Frank shouted. The sleek hitter raced for second base while the fielders came together to reach the ball.

"He's not stopping!" Michael jumped up from his seat.

Frank and the whole crowd around them stood up as the runner headed towards third base, coming right at them. The other team's second baseman received the ball from the outfielder and threw the ball like a dart at the outstretched glove of the third baseman.

"Dive!" Michael shouted as the runner dove headfirst towards the bag. The runner's arms were outstretched and attempted to touch it before the third baseman could tag him with the ball. The two players and ball came together at the base. The umpire hovered over them to make the call. There was a momentary hush in the crowd. The umpire dramatically spread his arms wide to indicate the runner was safe. The crowd roared in approval and they all high fived each other in celebration. The runner asked for timeout to stand up and dust himself off from all the dirt on his uniform from his slide. The crowd continued to applaud and then quieted down and sat back in their seats.

"There is nothing like a triple," Michael enthused. Frank took another sip of beer and looked at him. Michael emphatically threw his arms wide. "I mean, it is a beautiful, synchronized movement. The hitting of the ball. It being perfectly placed in a line drive between the fielders. The racing of the runner around the base paths. The way the defensive team coordinates itself to retrieve, throw, and catch the ball. It's just wonderful how all the forces come together in such a dramatic way."

Frank stared at Michael. "What? The guy hit the ball and ran like hell around the base paths while the other team fielded the ball and threw it to the infielder to get him out. That's it."

"No, no, it's a dance! It's just beautiful. I'm going to use that in my next piece."

Frank shook his head and smiled at Michael. He slapped him on the leg. "You sure that we're brothers?"

The next batter hit a long fly ball that was caught. The runner on third base tagged up and easily scored. Everyone stood up and high fived each other again.

As they sat down, Michael looked around the stadium. "God, I hate this dome. It's so artificial, the fake grass, the light. It's two in the afternoon. Baseball should be played outside."

The game continued.

"So, do Mom and Dad know?" Frank asked again.

"I told them last night."

"What did they say?"

Vendors walked up and down the long aisles in the stands offering hotdogs, beer, peanuts, popcorn, and Coke. Periodically, they would stop and make a sale and the whole row of people would get involved passing the food, drink and money back and forth.

Three years ago, Michael took his elderly grandmother to a game. His grandmother was a keen fan but rarely went to a live game. When asked if she wanted any food, his grandmother remarked, "I didn't come here to eat." The man next to Michael at this game seemed to order something every inning, and appeared to be getting bigger by the minute.

"Well, Mom was really upset, and I had a long talk with her," Michael said as he passed a hot dog. "In the end, she understood. She said she'd love to see London."

"And Dad?" Frank asked.

"He listened, then said, 'Huh.' And said no more.

"Typical." Frank finished his beer. "What about Jasper, is he going with you?"

Michael blew his cheeks out. "We split up a month ago."

"Oh, sorry." Frank hurriedly drank his beer and focused back out onto the field.

"I'm leaving next week." Michael cracked a peanut shell and popped the nut into his mouth. "I want to get settled in before the autumn season starts."

The eighth inning had finished, and the Twins took the field for hopefully the last time as they were now leading 5-3.

Frank continued to look out onto the field. "Well, I can't imagine those English folks wanting to watch a dance about baseball!"

Frank had never been to one of Michael's dance performances. His mother and sisters had, but the men in the family had always made their excuses.

The game ended. The Twins won, and the crowd emptied the stadium in a good mood. The brothers walked with the fans.

Frank threw his arm around Michael. "I'm going to miss you. One more beer before we say goodbye?"

Michael leaned into his brother. "Sure."

They strolled side by side down the street to a nearby tavern. Vendors tried to entice the happy parting crowd with the Twins' merchandise and the last remaining hot dogs and hamburgers from their stands. Once they got to the tavern, they pushed their way through the hordes of fans to the bar and ordered a couple of beers. Frank raised his bottle and clinked his with Michael's.

"Cheers! As they say in England," Frank said.

"Cheers!" Michael raised the bottle to his lips.

There was a buzz around them as the crowd drank and laughed with each other.

"My belly feels like a case of beer," Michael said, rubbing his stomach. "It's going to take two hard classes tomorrow to burn this off."

Frank looked down at his belly. "Mine is a keg of beer. It just keeps getting bigger." His stomach comfortably rolled over his belt buckle.

Michael patted it. "Oh, you're not in too bad a shape." Frank was six foot and broad. His biceps and chest muscles were big and well defined. His work kept him fit. Michael was slightly taller than Frank but lean and strong. Their square jaws, broad foreheads, and piercing, brown eyes made them look clearly related. Both had coarse, brown hair. Frank's was beginning to thin on top.

"Well, come to a week of my classes and we can burn it off for you," Michael said.

84

Frank grabbed a handful of French fries. "Yeah, right. I could see me in a pair of leotards like you wear."

Michael looked at him up and down. "Well, maybe not."

Frank finished his fries, then pushed the plate with the remaining mountain of fries away from him. "Well, maybe I'll lose a few pounds in the next year. A few of us hometown boys are looking at buying a big chunk of land up near Mom and Dad's cabin. A lot of untouched forest, a big swamp, and a small lake. We're going to build a hunting lodge. Use it for deer, duck and grouse hunting."

Michael slapped him on the back, "Sounds a dream come true for you, brother."

"Yeah, it's what I've wanted for years. Finally convinced Jim, Matt, and others to join me. We've a lot of work to do. It will take some time to get all the paperwork and finances sorted. But I can't wait to get started."

The tavern continued to fill with fans. The highlights of the game were being shown on televisions dotted around the building. People shouted in approval when the Twins scored a run or made a great defensive play. There was nothing like reliving a win.

The brothers finished their beers and slipped their way through the drunken crowd and out onto the street. They headed towards a bus stop as Michael lived in another part of the city. Frank parked his car nearby. He came in from the suburbs. When they got to the stop, they stood and looked at each other.

Frank put out his hand to shake. "Take care little brother, safe journey."

Michael ignored the handshake and gave his brother a quick hug. Tears came to his eyes and he brushed them away. "Yeah, I will," he said. "Please keep an eye on Mom. I know she said the hospital gave her the all clear, but breast cancer can come back."

Frank nodded. "Okay, will do."

The red bus pulled up to the stop.

Michael was about to get on the on when he turned and said, "And don't kill all the deer in the forest. Remember Bambi."

Frank smiled and punched him on the arm. "Get on the fuckin' bus."

Michael got on and paid his fare. As he sat down, he looked back. Frank stood with his hands in his pockets. Sunlight caught the tears on his rugged face.

Chapter 15

Florida. Spring, 1991.

Mary's walk slowed then came to an abrupt halt as she got to the door of the golf shop. Frank trailed behind her. He loitered, looking up, mesmerized by the swaying palms. He bumped into her and accidentally pushed her against the glass door.

"Hey, what's up?" he asked as he stood back.

Mary turned to him and put her finger to her lips.

Frank took a couple more steps back and stretched out his arms. "What?"

Mary peered inside. Standing in the middle of the shop was a tanned, athletic woman in her mid-forties. Rosalyn. Mary was to play an invitational round with her today with the prospect of joining the club.

"Damn," Mary muttered as she turned away. "I can't do this."

Frank put his hands out and stopped her from walking away. "You'll be fine."

"Oh, will I?" Mary's hands clenched as she tipped her head into Frank's chest.

"Of course you will. Golf. It's head down, swing through. Hit the ball. Simple."

Mary looked up and smirked. "What do you know about this stupid game?" She stood back and saw that Frank was already beginning to perspire heavily, even though it was only ten in the morning.

"Oh, Frankey. Look at you. I appreciate you coming down to visit. I know how much you hate hot weather."

Frank mopped his sweaty brow. "Well I wanted to see how my little sister was doing down here. Besides, it's March in Minnesota. The ice on the lakes is beginning to thaw, so no fishing. Can't hunt either. Nothing to do up there."

"Well, thanks, anyways." She glanced back at Rosalyn. "I better go."

Frank squeezed her shoulders. "Now get in there and kick her butt. I'll be back at the apartment. Call me later and I'll come back and pick you up."

"Okay, big brother."

Mary steadied herself, turned and walked briskly into the shop.

Three hours later, Frank got out of the car and opened the trunk. A young, tanned attendant in his crisp, white shorts and top put Mary's golf clubs in. Both Mary and Frank fumbled with their wallets to tip him but he just waved them away and hurried back to the clubhouse. They got into the car.

"So, how was that?" Frank asked.

Mary rolled down her window and lit a cigarette. "Well, better than I expected. She is going to propose me for membership. She is an important person at the club. Said I won't even need an interview by the committee. She is president."

"Well done! I could see you were very nervous."

Mary chuckled. "Yes, I was. But I hit my first drive right down the middle and she hit hers into the bushes. Mom would have been proud. After that I settled down." She didn't tell Frank that she had taken a valium beforehand to keep her calm.

"It was odd that Mom didn't play at all till all of us had left home," Frank said. "She was a county champion in her late teens and early twenties."

"Well, she took Anne and I to lessons. Remember?"

Frank turned out onto the highway. "I do. But looking back, I'm surprised she didn't pick it up when you did."

Mary finished her cigarette and stubbed it into the ashtray. "No time, I guess. The typical suburban American housewife in the fifties and sixties."

Frank noticed Mary fiddling with her wedding ring. "Still wearing the band, I see. Why is that, or have you secretly married?"

She punched him in the arm. "No chance." She had divorced Ralph three years ago. "I find it helpful in social situations. Keeps the wolves from circling me. I talk about my attentive husband and how he cares for our autistic twin boys."

"Oh, Mary, you are naughty!"

"Well, now that I got my nursing license back, maybe I'll take the ring off and make this attentive husband and the twins disappear." Mary pointed. "Take the second left up here and go to that fish shop. We can get some fish for tonight and you have to try their fish tacos for lunch. They are out of this world."

Frank indicated a left turn. "Now you're talking!"

Mary picked out some barracuda and scallops. Frank just nodded. He was already in rapture with the fish tacos and hot sauce.

Frank wiped his mouth. "Oh, my. I might just spend the rest of the day here. Especially if I had a cold beer or two."

"I'll tell you what," Mary said, "get a couple more tacos to take away, we'll pick up a few beers for you. You can drink them at the apartment. Then we both can have a little siesta."

Frank clapped his hands together. "Let's do it!"

That evening they sat out on the balcony of Mary's apartment with their meal of fish, salad and bread. Frank opened a bottle of cold beer. He clinked the bottle with Mary's glass of lemonade.

"To your health!" He looked out onto the sea. "Ah, this is very nice, sister. Look at that sunset!"

"Yes, I chose this place for them," Mary said. "I read somewhere that the happiest people are those that see sunsets most evenings."

Frank took a drink of his beer. "So, are you? Happy?"

Mary cut into her fish. "Yes, I'm getting there. I thought a lot of the reason that I took the drugs and alcohol was because of my back pain."

"How is that now?" Frank said. "You seem to be moving pretty well, and you're starting to play golf."

"Yes, it is much more manageable." Mary flexed her biceps. "I do daily yoga for the stretch and strength. It also calms me. I learned it in the detox center." Mary put some salad on her plate. "It was pain I was trying to avoid. But it wasn't physical pain." She pointed to her head and heart with her fork. "I was really unhappy in my marriage and with myself. It's been tough, but I'm getting there." She pointed her fork at Frank. "So what about you, big brother?"

"Oh no, no," Frank dug into his meal. "What was it Grandma used to say? Shut up and eat?" He kept his head down and continued to eat.

Mary leaned forward. "Ha! You think you can get away with it that easy? I've had a ton of therapy and group work. I know all the avoidance schemes."

Frank didn't make eye contact. "But the barracuda will get cold. Can't eat cold fish."

"You're a big boy. You can eat, swallow, then talk." Mary continued to stare at him. "So how is it going with Jenny and the boys?"

"Oh God." Frank squirmed in his chair. He took a quick swig of his beer. "She's fine. They're fine. I like her. A lot. But I don't want to live with her." He cut a piece of fish and shoved it into his mouth.

Mary smiled. "Now that wasn't too hard. Was it? Does she want to live with you?"

"Oh, Mary." Frank sighed. "Can we change the subject? I wanted to talk about Dad."

"Ah..." Mary sat back. "I'm going to let you off the hook. Is Dad okay?"

"Yes, he's okay. Well, sort of." Frank picked up his napkin and wiped his mouth.

Mary sat up. "Is he ill?"

Frank blew air out from his cheeks. "No, no. Nothing like that. I really want us all to get together for Christmas. Can you come up?"

Mary pushed back her chair. "Frankey. What's up? He went deer hunting with you this year. Did something happen?"

Frank took a swig from his beer. "Mary. We need to get together. All of us. To talk. Mikey couldn't come to Mom's funeral. I have spoken to him already and he says he could come over for Christmas."

Mary examined her brother closely and shook her head. "You're not telling me something." She reached for his beer but Frank grabbed her wrist.

He released her. "You're right, Mary. I'm not telling you something. But it is something that we all need to be together for."

Mary snorted. "Does Mikey know what you're not telling me?"

Frank took the beer and finished it. Then he put it on the table with a thud. "Nope. And neither does Anne."

Mary glared at him then took a deep breath. "Okay then, I'll come up for Christmas." She looked at the food on the table. "Now let's shut up and eat."

They both put their heads down and finished their meal in silence. The waves on the nearby beach crashed onto the rocks.

Chapter 16

Frank reached the end of the ridge and made his way into the forest. The snow continued to fall and the light was beginning to leave this day. Frank approached the edge of a small clearing. He heard the deep grunt of the buck and he stopped. He turned his head to see where the sound came from. There, fifty yards away in the clearing, were three deer. The big buck was jousting with a younger buck and a doe stood nearby. It wasn't a ferocious battle, rather a gentle wrestling match that a father might have with a son. The two continued to play while Frank stealthily moved closer to the edge of the clearing. He kept his eye on all of them, watching for the slightest sign of disturbance. They hadn't noticed him. Frank lifted the bow with his left arm and pulled the string taut. The arrow was ready to launch. He waited while the deer continued to spar. The doe moved between him and the big buck.

"Dammit, move," Frank muttered to himself.

His right arm was beginning to ache from holding the string back. He relaxed his grip, allowing the bow to dip. The big buck stopped wrestling and looked up. It lifted its nose into the air and moved towards the woods. The doe and other buck now stood behind him. Steam rose off the hide of the powerful buck as it breathed in its surroundings. Its black eyes looked into the trees for danger. Frank forced himself not to blink or breath. His whole body became rigid. Light snowflakes continued to fall in the silent wood. Frank knew that it was now or never. He would have to breathe soon. The buck would notice the steam and flee.

In one quick precise movement, Frank lifted the bow and pulled back the string. He aimed and shot his arrow at the buck. A dull thud sounded as the arrow hit the chest of the animal and sank deep into its flesh. The buck's eyes opened wide as its body shuddered from the impact of the arrow. Its shoulders buckled and it staggered to hold itself upright. Frank pulled another arrow out and fired it at the beast. It struck it in the neck. Blood spurted from the incision. The buck groaned and fell to its knees. Its head dropped and it fell to the ground crushing the snow beneath it. The buck's body violently thrashed for a minute and then lay still. The great stag lay dead in the snow, surrounded by a pool of bright red blood. The other deer stood still for a moment then fled into the nearby woods. The forest was silent again. Steam continued to rise from the big buck's carcass.

Frank stood motionless at the edge of the clearing, looking at the buck. He could feel his heart pounding in his chest. His bow and arrows had dropped to the ground. His breathing was shallow and little steam clouds rose from his nose.

He closed his eyes and thought to himself, *It couldn't get better than this.* He had hunted the whole day. His shot was precise. The death was sudden and with minimal pain.

Frank moved from among the trees and stood over his prey. The blood which surrounded the carcass was beginning to deepen in color as it coagulated. He bent down to touch the animal. It was warm but still. Frank could smell the overpowering odor of the buck emanating from its hide. It made him gag and he had to turn his head away. He gathered himself and then pulled out his long hunting knife. He would have to gut the animal before dragging it out of the woods. Frank strained to turn the buck onto its back. With the knife, he made a deep incision from the top of the ribcage to the end of the belly. Heat poured out of the stomach as its contents seeped out onto the ground. Again, Frank turned his head away to avoid the stench. He held his breath as he took off his gloves and put his hands inside the warm carcass to pull out the remaining organs. He then wiped off as much blood as he could from his hands and knife and into the snow. He stood back and looked at the animal. It was magnificent.

It was getting dark and he would have to move quickly before night fell upon the forest. He hurriedly went back to gather up his bow and quill before returning to the stag. He groaned as he lifted the buck's giant antlers and began to drag the deer out of the woods. A trail of blood followed him as he slowly slid the buck across the snow. He knew he would have to hurry because soon the wolves would pick up the scent and start to follow him. Within a few minutes, the weight of the beast was already beginning to bear down on him.

"Come on, Frankey." He took a deep breath. "Keep moving, keep moving."

Chapter 17

The priest's car turned off the dirt road into the cemetery which was set on the outskirts of the old mining town. The cars behind followed. They wound their way up the snow-plowed lane and stopped in front of a hole that was covered by a large green mat. A mound of soil lay next to it. The ground was so deeply frozen that it had to be heated before it could be dug out by a yellow digger. The digger was now parked discretely in the corner of the cemetery. Next to it was a car with the two gravediggers. They turned their engine off as the entourage pulled up next to the grave. The car doors all seemed to open at once as the priest and the family got out and moved to the plot. Michael noticed that the gravestones in the vicinity of the open grave all bore the same name, his: 'BRESLIN'. Grandparents, uncles, aunts, cousins, and his mother were all buried here. His grandparents on his father's side had immigrated from Germany in the late 1800s.

Father Benedict stood over the grave. The urn had been placed on a low table in front of it. The family formed a tight group behind the priest. Mary pushed her body into Michael and he put his arm around her. He drew her close to him.

"In the name of the Father, Son, and Holy Ghost," the priest began. Those of the family who still practiced dutifully made the sign of the cross. Michael and other non-believers bowed their heads and closed their eyes while the priest proceeded through the burial ritual. The young altar boy shivered in his thin cloak as he stood next to the priest.

Peter stood apart from the group and stared at the urn. The dog lay at his feet. He had lost his wife and now his favorite son. He was like one of the pike he used to catch. Peter had been caught with the jagged hook of life. He was then surgically gutted with a sharp steel knife. His entrails laid on a table and his startled eyes stared coldly into the distance. He was desperate for a drink – a three-fingered measure of his favorite Scottish whisky with a little ice.

The two boys pressed hard into both sides of their mother. Their eyes were closed shut and the younger one put his gloved hand to his ears to prevent the priest's words from entering. Jenny's knees were shaking and she looked like a tree about to fall. The boys leant into her and she held them tightly, and the three managed to keep standing.

The late afternoon cold pushed the whole group closer together. The priest took a metal vessel from the altar boy and sprinkled holy water over the urn.

"For dust thou art, and onto dust thou shall return." He then made the sign of the cross.

The service was over. No one moved. The silence and cold fused together to hold them in a vacuum. A muffled cry broke the silence. It was Mary. Her was face buried into Michael's chest and he held her tight. The boys stared at Mary and began to cry. Jenny gathered them up and steered them back towards the car. Her body stiffened as she tried to hold back her tears, her grief. The boys had to be cared for. Her time would come later.

Anne, accompanied by Marco, solemnly walked back with the priest towards his car. There, they would collect the other urn to take to the hunting lodge.

"Thank you again for coming to the gravesite, Father," Anne said.

They stopped in front of Sally's grave. Father Benedict took her hand. "It is the least I could do for your family. You have had a lot of loss to deal with."

He made the sign of the cross over her grave then walked towards the car. The driver stood at attention next to the open back door. Father Benedict gave a last wave at Anne then slid into the backseat. The driver slammed the door then hurriedly went around the car and got in himself. The altar boy jumped into the front seat. The cold engine started with a roar and crawled away from the burial site. Once it passed out of the cemetery, the car accelerated and began its long journey back to the city.

Michael took Mary to their car. The rest of the group made their way to their cars and started them up. Peter and the dog remained motionless at the burial site. Michael got Mary in the car and started the engine. Then he went back to the site.

Michael stood next to his father for a moment in silence. "Dad?" he whispered. The dog looked up and wagged his tail. "Dad. It's time to go now." Peter continued to stare at the urn.

"This wasn't supposed to happen," Peter said.

"I know, Dad."

"You should never bury your kids. It just isn't right." Peter began to cry. "It was bad enough to bury Sally. But this."

Peter's body crumpled into a heap. Michael moved quickly to catch him and hold him up. The startled dog jumped out of the way and stared at them.

"Dad." Peter was sobbing into his chest. Michael shifted his body and took the weight of his sagging father. He allowed his father to cry for several minutes. Finally, Peter stopped. They stood quietly together in the cold barren graveyard.

"Come on, Dad, we have to go now."

He turned his father away from the gravesite and guided

them back towards the car. The dog trailed behind them. After a few steps, Peter suddenly stopped. He shook, freeing himself from Michael's hold.

"Leave me alone!" Peter muttered angrily.

Michael stood back, startled. "I was just trying to help."

"Don't need your help," he bristled as he glared at the ground. Peter then turned to the dog. "Come on, Max. Let's get back to the car." Peter and the dog shuffled back to Anne's car. Michael sighed and had one last look at the grave. He then made his way to the car where Mary sat, slumped in the front seat.

Chapter 18

Jerry stood at the door of the lodge and scanned the woods.

"I wonder where Frankey is?" Ice-cold air rushed at his face. "He should be getting back soon. It's almost dark out there."

"Will you shut the frigging door!" Alex shouted from the card table. "He'll be back soon. Shut that door!"

Jerry took one last look into the twilight and closed the door.

Four of the men sat around the card table playing poker. Jim lay on his bed trying to sober up for the upcoming evening drinking session.

Alex fiddled with his cards and then proudly displayed them on the table, saying, "Read them and weep, boys. Two pair. Aces high." He laughed while the others groaned. His fat hands stretched out over the table to collect the winnings. Once he had piled all the chips into neat little stacks, he leaned back and blew a cloud of cigar smoke into the air. "You know, boys, I've been thinking. Fuck bows and arrows!" He looked around the room at all the stuffed deer and moose heads on the wall. He held up an imaginary gun in his hands. "Boom!" he shouted. "Boom! Boom! Boom!" His arms moved from head to head. "I love to nail those buggers."

"Ya, right. The big hunter," Jim said from his bed. "Have you got off that fat ass of yours yet today?" He glared at Alex. Then he rolled over and said, "Deal the cards and shut up."

Frank stopped and laid the buck in the snow. He was beginning to perspire heavily and he opened the collar of his jacket to cool off. He looked up into the dark blue sky and could see the first stars coming out. The cold air quickly began to find openings in his clothing and attack his body. He had been dragging the deer for forty minutes and he was now near the truck. His back and shoulders were aching but he didn't care. The adrenaline of the hunt and kill was still racing through him. It would probably keep him awake all night as he sat around with his buddies in the lodge, celebrating his conquest. He could see all of them standing at the door of the lodge as he pulled in with his truck and the big buck strapped to the roof. A sharp cracking sound in the woods behind him made him think of the wolves again. He glanced at the woods then stooped down to pick up the antlers and made his way towards the truck.

When Frank got to the road, he saw his truck covered in snow. The flow of blood from the deer had stopped and the carcass had begun to stiffen. He brought the deer up to the side of the truck and dropped it in exhaustion. He pulled out the keys to the truck from his pocket and opened the cab door. The inside was littered with empty bottles and sandwich wrappers. There was a strong smell of stale cigar smoke. He sat behind the wheel and turned the key. The motor grumbled and stopped. Frank turned the key again. The engine turned over twice, coughed, and quit. "Come on, baby," Frank said to the truck, as he massaged the gas pedal. He waited a minute and tried again. The motor coughed, protested, and then came to life with a groan. "Yes!" Frank shouted.

He got out of the truck and scraped the snow off the roof. Behind the seat he had a coil of rope and he brought it out to tie the deer. Frank looked down at the buck. Its eyes were glazed over and its pale tongue hung out of the side of the mouth. He brought the two front hooves together and tied them securely. He did the same with the back legs. The stiff carcass was heavy and awkward to lift and Frank grunted loudly as he hoisted it onto the truck. A few remaining internal juices seeped out from the buck. Frank made the final adjustments to the deer before he secured its legs to the front and back of the truck with the rope. He stood back and pulled out a cigar and looked at his conquest. Its head and huge rack of antlers hung over the windscreen like a maidenhead of a ship. Frank lifted his head and blew the cigar smoke into the night air. He again thought of the men standing in amazement at the door of the lodge as he drove in with the buck. He hated to admit it to himself, but for all the purity of the hunt and the kill, their respect was still very important to him. He grinned and blew some more cigar smoke into the air. He excitedly jumped into the seat of his truck and slammed the door. He revved the engine and drove the truck up the small road and out of the woods.

The going was slow due to the amount of snow and ice. The headlights of the truck bounced off the trees at the side of the road. He would be able to speed up once he reached the plowed highway a mile further up the road. Frank leaned over and turned on the radio. Tammy Wynette was belting out 'Stand by Your Man'. "Yeah, right." Frank said to himself. He started to sing along and thought about Rita. They had been married two years. She was tall and thin, with jet black hair. He met her at a Plumbing and DIY show. She was a sales representative for a plastics firm. Frank could never figure out women and so he had always kept his distance. But she was different, and he knew it.

With a big laugh and a firm body, he couldn't resist himself. He bought four hundred dollars' worth of plastic piping he would never use and a date for the next evening. She was easy to talk to and made him laugh a lot. Within two months, she had moved into his small two-bedroom house by the river on the outskirts of town. She let him hunt and sometimes she went fishing with him. And they had wonderful times in bed. But after two years it didn't work for Frank. He didn't want to have to talk every night when he came home from work. Sometimes he just wanted a beer and a ball game. Was that too much to ask? She got lonely and after a while lost her laugh. When he rejected the idea of having children, she slid away. He took a deep breath. He could still see her face and hear that laugh.

Jenny with her two boys had come into his life unexpectedly. He had fixed their central heating and stayed around for dinner. He liked how they lived separately. He sensed that soon she was going to pop the question of them living together. He wasn't so sure about becoming a father, let alone a husband again.

The truck reached the highway. It turned right onto the road and into the darkness. He put on the high beams of the truck. His foot slammed the gas pedal to the floor. He knew that he would be back at the lodge in a few minutes. The truck sped down the empty highway.

A slow mournful tune came on the radio. He looked at the radio and chomped on his cigar. "Screw that crap! Let's have some music!" He turned the dial of the radio through a few channels till he came to Hank Williams singing 'Honky Tonk Blues'. "Now that's more like it!" Frank laughed, and blew more cigar smoke into the cab. He was ready to party with his buddies. A few snowflakes landed on the windscreen. The truck began to climb a small hill. Frank threw his head back and sung out with the music. "Honkeeey Tonkin!"

He got to the top of the hill and looked down the road. His whole body suddenly tensed. A hundred yards ahead of him, a doe had moved out on the road followed by another deer. They stood blinded by the headlights. His hands gripped the steering wheel. "Move!" he yelled at them. "Get out of the way!" They stood paralyzed in the light. The truck hurtled towards them. Frank's jaw clamped onto the cigar. He thrust his foot onto the brake and immediately the truck began to swerve left and right on the icy road. His hands clung to the wheel to try and control its slide.

"Move! Move!" he shouted. Both deer stood frozen in front of him. Steam rose from their hides. "No! No!" he screamed. Frank turned the wheel sharply to the right and the tires screeched. The truck plowed through a small snowbank at the roadside and hurtled towards the forest. Frank gripped the steering wheel. He saw the trees come towards him. His body tensed and then became silent. He closed his eyes. The truck slammed into the base of a large pine tree. The front of the truck crumpled upon impact. Frank's body flew forward onto the steering wheel crushing his ribcage and instantly tearing his aorta in two. Blood rushed from his open chest. His head and body jerked back and forth. His eyes opened and looked up for a moment. He grunted and he took a shallow breath. His neck flopped forward and his eyes closed. Blood continued to pour out of his chest. His body quivered and shook. His hands clenched and then went limp. A last breath left his body.

The truck lay at the foot of the pine. Its headlights stayed on and the radio was blaring music into the silent forest. The big buck had been thrown forward by the impact and laid on the crumpled front hood of the truck. The two deer stood for a moment on the road above him. They then left the road and made their way into the woods.

An hour later, Jim stood in the doorway of the lodge. He

looked into the darkness and could see headlights making their way up the road to the lodge.

"Hey, here he comes," Jim shouted to the other men. "Here comes, Frankey Buck!"

The men got up from the poker table and walked to the door. The police car turned into the driveway of the hunting lodge. Its high beams caught the startled faces of the men.

Chapter 19

Once the funeral had finished, all the men drove up to the hunting lodge. They had arrived an hour ago. A light snowfall had dusted the whole wooded landscape. The sky was clear but more snow was forecast for later. They had left the family to bury half the ashes in the family grave. The other half would be scattered on the grounds of the hunting lodge tomorrow. The large red snowblower was started. Harry, a burly garage mechanic, got behind it and moved it along, shifting snow from the parking area. The overweight Alex and Jim grabbed shovels and cleared the walkways. Bob grabbed a broom and swept the outside stairs to the balcony, which he then cleared. Jerry and Matt unloaded the cars and turned the heating on in the lodge. Once all of these tasks were completed, each was given a job to prepare for the family's arrival.

"What time should we expect them?" Jim asked while he unpacked the food.

Bob, who was the main cook, said, "They left soon after the brunch. The service at the cemetery will be short. And then they'll come right here. I suppose about six." It was five o'clock now.

Harry walked by with the bed linen. "Hey Bob, whatya going to make for them and us?"

Bob ran a local gas station in the town where they all lived. His size indicated he loved his food. "Just a big game stew, Frankey's favorite. And some bread, salad."

Harry nodded. "Sounds great. Remember, there might be a vegetarian or two."

Alex opened a beer. "Yeah, I think his funky niece is one and his fag brother."

"Hey. None of that," Bob said.

Harry turned to Alex. "Yeah, none of that. And I thought we all agreed not to drink till they got here."

"Yeah," Jim said. "Remember? We'll see what they want to do. Maybe there'll be no drinking tonight."

Alex looked at them and then at the beer. "Okay then." He took a quick swig and poured the rest down the sink. "Well, if they don't drink here, once we get them settled we can go down to the shack." The men nodded in agreement.

"I can't see Frankey's dad not wanting a drink," Jerry said.

"Right!" Jim clapped his hands together. "Let's get moving. They'll be here soon."

A hum of activity filled the lodge. Beds were made, bathrooms were cleaned, the dining table was set and food was prepared. Alcohol bottles and glasses were lined up, just in case. The lights were dimmed and music was turned off. The smell of the meat and vegetable stews dominated the room. Once finished, the men sat around the table drinking coffee and talked quietly to one another. A hand painted sign that normally hung in the center of the dining room saying 'WHATEVER HAPPENS AT THE LODGE, STAYS AT THE LODGE' was taken down and put away from public view.

Matt, who ran their local liquor store, a bald, bearded man with thick arms, spoke up. "Boys, I think we have to be very careful what we say to Frankey's family tonight. I've had a word with Ray's son Eddy, who is now running the tavern over there in Twin Pines. He said some Indians were making a bit of noise about a couple of half-breed kids growing up on the reservation. They say they are ours."

"Sheeeit." Jerry whistled.

Alex pounded his fist on the table. "How they goin' ta prove that?"

"Indians said someone here was paying money to the mothers," Matt said. "You know some of the women there don't have men."

Alex jumped up and looked around the table. "Who'd do that?"

The men looked at him and then at one another. It hit them all at the same moment. Alex sat down.

"Ah shit," Jim said.

Jerry looked up at the ceiling. "Sheeit indeed, brother."

A horn from one of the family's car could be heard as they approached. They all turned towards the door.

"They're here," Harry said as he stood up.

"Not a word, boys," Matt barked. "We'll sort this out later."

The wooden floor gave out a high squeak as they hurriedly pushed their chairs away in unison and stood to attention. They all glanced from one to the other. No one moved.

Jim broke the silence. "Come on, boys. Let's do Frankey proud!"

They grouped together and patted each other on the shoulders. Then they made their way towards the headlights and the front door.

Chapter 20

Anne was the last of the four children to leave home. When she left, a huge space was created in Sally's life, like a sinkhole that develops overnight. It was now just Peter, the dog, and her. None of her children had left the Minneapolis area. Michael was in the heart of the city, while the others were settled in other suburbs to the south and west. They all came and visited at the appropriate times, but clearly their focus was outwards and away from this home that Sally had so lovingly created.

Sally normally stayed in bed when Peter rose in the morning to go to work. When she woke an hour later, she'd go into the living room where she would be greeted by the smell of stale cigarette smoke and coffee. She'd survey the room, sigh and begin to clean up. Next to Peter's old brown armchair, she would clear the colony of cigarette butts. They were stubbed into the turquoise ashtray that they had bought while on holiday in New Mexico. On this occasion, she picked up the stained red coffee cup and collected the morning newspaper that was strewn on the carpet. Barney, their ten-year-old Irish Setter, laid in the middle of the mess and wagged his tail in anticipation of breakfast. Peter had let him out to urinate in the morning, but only gave him a little treat. He never fed the dog. Sally gave Barney his breakfast of tinned dog food and biscuits and then had a cup of coffee herself. After that, she took a shower.

It was mid-February. She had plans for the garden and the golf course would soon be open. The warm water streamed down over her head as she soaped her sagging arms, legs and body. She raised her right armpit and rubbed the soap against the skin. The soap felt like it had broken up into a few pieces in her hand. She looked at the soap and saw it was intact. She froze then dropped the soap. It hit the shower floor with a dull thud. Sally closed her eyes. Water poured over her head for a minute. She took a deep breath and lifted her arm. She felt the firm nodules embedded into the skin underneath. Five of them. Her head and shoulders dropped as she slumped in the shower. Tears gushed from her eyes. They joined the water from above, creating a small pool at her feet.

"Oh no," she groaned.

This time the cancer didn't let her go. It ravaged her body and no medicine could stop it. She died in the late spring. The garden sat overgrown and unattended. No one in the family could bear to go out in it.

After Sally died, Peter began to drink as soon as he got home from work. By early evening four empty bottles of beer would lie at his feet as he stared out into the garden. Mary and Anne came twice a week with precooked meals for their father. Peter could cook but didn't see the point. He pushed their food around the plate, ate a few mouthfuls then gave the rest to an eager Barney, who sat expectantly by his side. Every day his morning alarm clock rattled his hungover brain. He stopped shaving and a coarse beard speckled with black and grey whiskers sprung up on his tired face. For the next six months he forced himself to keep going into work. He drove aimlessly from one project to another, delegating as much responsibility as he could to eager subordinates. Then he would go home to his dog and a refrigerator full of beer.

One Saturday afternoon, he sat half listening to the football game on the radio. He struggled to push himself up out of his armchair and staggered into the kitchen to fetch another beer. He caught his image in the living room mirror. An old haggard man stood before him. Peter was aghast. He stopped and looked long and hard into the mirror.

"Nah. That's enough," he said to himself. "Come on. Let's move on." He went upstairs and it took him twenty minutes to shave his face clean of the beard. Then he took a long shower. He scrubbed hard all over his body. He finished by turning the shower freezing cold and stood under the torrent of water for three minutes. He then came out of the shower and briskly dried himself with a towel.

Peter decided at that moment to take early retirement. He was sixty-two. Now that Sally was gone and the children had left there was nothing holding him to this suburban life. He sold the house. The children came and took some of the contents for their own homes or for sentimental value. Most of the rest he sold or gave away. He packed up a few remaining items and moved to the cabin on the lake. This was where his children and Sally had spent a lot of time and he has spent little time. Peter was back up on the Iron Range with his kind of people. He quickly became the local handyman in the area, and the rest of the time he hunted and fished. Frank invited his father to the lodge to deer hunt with him and his gang that following November. Normally, Peter hunted with his two older brothers and their boys, but this was an opportunity to go to the lodge and hunt with his son. They built a deer stand on the edge of a clearing in the summer. When they hunted in November, Peter would go to this stand and wait, while Frank and others would walk noisily through the woods from the opposite side of their land. This would move the deer towards the stand. Hiding there, Peter could easily shoot the unsuspecting deer.

November came and they agreed to meet at Ray's Tavern in the early evening. Frank came from Minneapolis and Peter from his cabin.

Peter was sitting at the bar when Frank arrived. An empty bottle of beer sat before him. A college football game was being shown on the television overhead. A few other older men in baseball hats and plaid shirts were scattered around the dimly-lit bar.

"Hey, son." Peter waved his hand when he saw Frank enter the bar. Frank ambled over. He was still wearing his grey overhauls that he wore to work. His name was embroidered in red above the pocket on his chest and 'BRESLIN PLUMBING' was on the back.

"Tough day?" his dad asked.

"Yeah, kind of. Squeezed two days' work into one, so I could get up here early." His hands still had a residue of grime and dirt on them.

"Well, you made it," Peter smiled. "Cold beer?"

"I could kill one."

Peter hailed the bartender. "Hey, Ray. A couple of Grain Belts for me and my son." He slapped Frank on the back. "This is Frankey, my boy."

Ray nodded to Frank and got the beers.

They clinked the bottles together and both drank them with gusto. Peter ordered a couple more.

"Ray does the best steaks in the area," Peter said. "Let's have a couple."

Frank looked around the bar and then at his dad. "How do you know this place?"

Peter's open smile pulled in at the sides. His eyes tightened at the edges. "Oh, I broke down a long time ago going up to the lake. Had to stay over. And I stayed here. They have some rooms at the back." His eyes darted around the room. They then returned to Frank. "How about those steaks?"

Frank studied his father for a moment. "Sure."

They moved over to a table near the juke box and sat down. They drank their beers and watched the football game. In a few minutes a young Indian woman brought out the steaks with potatoes.

"Hi Peter," she said. Then turned away.

Frank noticed his father's concealed smile. Peter's eyes followed the woman's ass as she walked away. They ate the steaks and talked about the next few days of hunting. The weather looked good. There was no new snow forecast, clear skies, but a cold northeast wind.

"I hope you have a few layers of thermals, Dad. It's going to be cold, and you'll have to sit quietly in that stand for at least a couple of hours before you might see any deer."

"No problem." Peter had been waiting for this opportunity for months. A bit of cold weather wasn't going to put him off. He was hoping he'd get a chance to shoot a big deer. Bring it down. Then bask in the respect of Frankey's friends. He didn't want to be the old man who was being dragged along. He was still a hunter.

They finished their meals. They then each had a shot of whisky.

"The lodge is about a twenty-mile drive from here, Dad. Think you can do it?" Frank sat back in his chair and studied his father. "We can leave your car here and collect it in the morning."

Peter raised his head to the ceiling and yawned. He closed

his eyes and shook his head. "Nah. You know, I'm kinda tired out from the drive. And too many beers. Think I'll stay here tonight. Remember? They have rooms." He glanced up at Frank. "You should stay here too."

Frank stretched his arms out. "No, I want to get to the lodge, heat it up good before the other guys arrive."

"Suit yourself," Peter said.

They paid the bill then went out to Peter's car. Frank helped him take his bag back to the room. It was plain space; dull brown wallpaper, a toilet next to a room with a double bed and thick quilts. A red lampshade emitted a low yellow light from the bedside table.

"Thanks for the help, Frank. Think I'll go back for a nightcap. Like one?"

"No, I've had enough. Better get going."

They patted each other on the shoulder and back. Frank strode off to his truck. Peter watched him get into the truck and waved. Then he made his way back to the bar. Frank got into his truck, revved up the motor and moved out onto the highway. He turned the radio on and quickly found a local station. The truck's headlights cut into the black night. He sat back in his seat and got comfortable for the drive.

He was five miles out, "Ah, shit." Frank said to himself.

They had left his father's rifle sitting in the back seat of the car. It was partially hidden, but if left overnight the car could get broken into and Peter would lose it. Frank checked his rear-view mirror and slowed down. The road was empty. There was a driveway ahead, marked by a silver mailbox. He signaled and used the side road to turn around. Once turned, he put foot to the floor and sped back to the bar. The car park was nearly empty, just three lonely cars waiting in the cold for their owners. He pulled up next his father's car and screeched to a halt. Frank jumped out of the truck and hurried towards the bar to get his dad's keys. He yanked the bar door open into the dark, smokey room. He looked around the bar. There at the far end of the counter was Peter with his arm around the waitress.

Frank stopped abruptly and stepped back into a dark corner and watched. Peter continued to talk to the waitress. They had a little laugh. Then he drew the woman closer to him and said something in her ear. She looked at him and nodded. She took off her apron and put it behind the counter. Peter stood up from the stool, had a quick glance around the bar, then escorted her out the back door. He didn't see Frank in the dark corner. Frank leaned back against the wall. He hesitated and shook his head. He covertly left by the front door and hurried around the back. There he saw his father, with his hand firmly on the woman's ass, enter the room. Frank tucked into the shadows and watched his father take a last look around before he closed the door. The blinds were drawn. Frank stared at the door for a few minutes. Then he stealthily slipped out the shadows and went back to his truck. He started the engine, put the truck into gear, and rolled out onto the deserted highway.

Chapter 21

The men from the lodge waited at the front door and watched as the cars came off the highway. Jim stood in the cleared space, waved his arms like an attendant on an airstrip and directed the drivers where to park. Once stopped, the car doors flew open and Frankey's dog bounded into the lot. The two boys tumbled out and raced after him. The men came out to help the rest of the family unload. They greeted each other in muffled voices. The boys' laughter and dog barking cut through the solemn air. It was decided earlier that the family would take the downstairs; Mary and Gina sharing, Michael and his father, Marco and Anne, with Jenny and the boys taking the other bedroom. The men would spread out in the living area, free bedrooms, and the shack. Only Peter had visited the lodge in the past. The family all went to their rooms and unpacked. After a short period, they all came upstairs and gathered in the dining area with the men. No one seemed to know what to do.

Finally, Jim cleared his throat in the awkward silence. "We'd like to welcome you all to our lodge." He paused for moment while everyone turned to look at him. "This was Frankey's dream and we helped him build it. With all due respect to everyone here, I think this is where Frankey felt most at home." Jenny's eyes flickered in acknowledgement as she nodded.

"Michael, that was a beautiful speech you gave at the funeral about how you two grew up together. I, or any of us, could never match that."

Michael stood with Mary leaning into him. "It's not a competition, Jim."

Jim smiled. "No. I guess it ain't."

Standing in the corner, Matt added, "Frankey was the real spirit of this place."

Jerry pointed at the wall. "Yeah, look at all those fuc... I mean friggin' deer and moose heads around here. They are almost all Frankey's."

The family looked up at all the animal trophies on the wall.

"Those stuffed pike, too!" Alex said.

"So. All I'm sayin," Jim's voice was beginning to crack, "Is that this lodge is a shrine to him. A church. A temple. He'll never be forgotten by us. His hunting pals."

There was a moment of silence followed by a round of applause.

"Now, there's food all ready for you!" Bob called out. "We have game and vegetarian stew! Come and eat!"

The family and men turned and started to move towards the pans of food and plates.

"Wait!" Peter spoke up. "I have something to say." Everyone stopped and looked at him.

Peter took a deep breath. "I could kill for a drink!"

The room erupted in laughter.

"That's music to my ears," Alex chirped. "What'll you have, Peter?"

Peter stuck three, then a fourth finger up. "Four fingers of whisky. Your best, with a little ice."

"Coming right up!" Alex said as he rushed towards the makeshift bar.

"Anyone else?" Matt asked.

Everyone in the family was desperate for a drink. They gave

their orders as they sat down with their plates of stew at the large wooden table. No one had eaten since breakfast. Anne pushed back her chair, stood up, and cleared her throat. She wanted to say grace before they began to eat. No one looked up at her. Red-faced, she quickly sat down again. Everyone around the table kept their heads down and devoured the meal.

Bob proudly stood by his pots of stew. "Come on up, don't be shy. We have loads more." The boys immediately jumped up and brought their plates to Bob. The dog followed behind wagging his tail ever hopeful for a scrap or two. Peter and Marco were right up after the boys, and soon everyone took their empty plates up to Bob. Matt and Jerry replenished everyone's drink. Once finished, Alex and Jim went around collecting all the dirty dishes. They began to look at each other and soon they were competing, trying to create the highest stack.

Matt saw what was going on. He stood up and lifted his hands into the air. "Whoa! Ladies, gentlemen, children and dog." Everyone stopped talking and stood to attention. "This is the final of the plate-stacking competition! To my right we have the defending champion, Mr. James Peterson, and to the left, the upstart Mr. Alexander Risconni."

The two men took their bows to howls of laughter and taunting from all in the room. Everyone was drinking freely.

Matt went over to them. "So the rules are clear. The highest stack to the kitchen sink in the shortest time." He counted Jim's stack. "Fourteen! Ready… and go!"

Jim lent down carefully and nestled the dirty plates against his chest. He turned and rushed to the sideboard next to the sink. Bob counted the seconds out loud. Jim eased the plates down on the counter and raised his arms in victory. Everyone cheered, the dog barked, they stomped their feet, and raised their glasses.

"Eighteen seconds!" Matt howled. The group quieted. Matt then turned to Alex's stack and counted them. "Wow, twenty-two plates! Can he do it?"

Everyone stood up and began to chant, "Alex! Alex!" This startled the dog and he started to bark again.

Alex readied himself and, on the word go, he lunged towards the plates. Everyone cheered him on.

The stack listed as he lifted the plates but he hurriedly turned and began to run towards the sink, while Bob shouted out the numbers. As he passed the table, the top plates began to slide.

"Whoa! Lookout!" Alex shrieked as he tried to control the plates. Two of the men jumped back, but this excited the dog and it jumped into Alex's path.

"Looko..." Alex and the dog collided. The dog yelped and ran to a corner, while Alex hit the floor with a thud. The plates flew in all directions and seemed to hang in the air before crashing to the ground and shattering in hundreds of pieces. Before anyone could help Alex, he jumped up, grabbed an unbroken plate and raced to the sink. "Finished!" he threw his arms out wide. The group clapped and hooted in approval.

Matt put an arm up and everyone became quiet. "Although Jim got his plates intact to the sink in the shortest time, I have to declare Alex the winner due to sheer grit and determination. Now, let's clean this mess up and keep drinking!" Everyone cheered and began to help the clean-up.

Once the last of the pieces of plate were cleared, Michael found a bottle of red wine. He looked at the label and grimaced at Mary. "Oh my, this looks dangerous." He showed it to her. "Kangarouge. An Australian Shiraz with a bit kick, it says."

"Shut up and open it." Mary swayed and crossed her arms to steady herself. "And let's have a glass."

Michael pointed a scolding finger at her. "Hey. No drugs, no alcohol."

"Just open the bloody bottle," Mary said. "That's how they say it over there? Bloody bottle?"

Michael laughed. "Yeah, bloody bottle." He opened the wine bottle and poured her a small glass.

Mary glared at the glass. "Keep going. I'll tell you when to stop."

Michael poured it practically to the top.

Mary put her hand up. "That'll do. To start."

Marco and Jerry came over to them, holding beers.

"Mikey…" Marco slurred, as he affectionately grabbed Michael by the arm. "Settle a bet. Jerry says it is quicker to fly from London to Minneapolis than Minneapolis to London."

They both held inquisitive drunken looks as they leaned in towards Michael.

"How much was the bet?" Michael asked.

"Ten bucks." Jerry grinned.

"Well, get out your wallet, Jerry," Michael said. "It's generally faster by an hour. Minneapolis to London. Because of the jet stream, a prevailing west to east air current."

"Yes!" Marco pumped his fist in the air.

Jerry pulled out his wallet and reluctantly gave Marco a ten-dollar bill. He grabbed it and waved it above him. Across the room, Anne looked at him disapprovingly.

Waving a bottle of beer, Matt said, "Hey, let's take this party downstairs!" Harry and Bob clinked their glasses in agreement, and the whole group began to move like a conga dance to the lower floor. Alex put the stereo on with Country Western music. Peter sat down on the sofa next Jenny. The two boys were dancing like a couple of drunken cowboys in the open space near the pool table. Three of the men brought down all of the alcohol.

Michael was talking to Bob and Jim when Gina playfully punched him from behind. He turned and she grabbed his free hand. She was swaying with a wry smile on her face.

"Come on, Uncle Mike! Let's dance!" She pulled him along towards a free space. Michael rolled his eyes, but found a place to put his drink and started to move his hips to the music. Gina moved around him as she extravagantly waved her arms and gyrated her body.

He moved closer to her. "How much have you had to drink?"

"Not enough!" she said as she continued to dance around him.

Marco had his hands on his hips and was strutting to the music. Anne stood next to him and shuffled her feet while watching her drunken daughter. Jerry grabbed Jenny and brought her out onto the dance floor. He said something into her ear. She shyly laughed, her body relaxed and began to dance with him. Mary moved out to dance with Bob. The other men stood around the makeshift bar. Peter sat on his own sofa and swirled his drink in his glass as everyone danced around him. He didn't want to party, but felt he couldn't just go sit in his room. So he just sat and waved his glass in the air for periodic refills.

After a few songs, Michael, who was now dancing with Mary, said to her, "Let's stop this crying-in-your-beer music. Put on some funk." He went over to the stereo and looked through the record collection. He found a Stevie Wonder album and put it on.

"Oh, yes!" Marco gestured for Michael to dance with him. Michael hesitated. He glanced at the men by the bar. They were all laughing and cajoling one another. Michael took a quick drink of his wine and then went out on the floor and began to dance with Marco. The men watched for a minute. They looked at one another. A couple of them cried out with their arms raised in the air. Then all of them rushed to the floor and began to dance. The next hour was a free-for-all. Everyone wildly danced with everyone else to loud funk and soul music. Peter continued to sit and drink.

The final song was played and then people began to say goodnight and go to their bedrooms. Gina was outside vomiting and Mary attended to her. Marco grabbed Anne and it was clear he was not taking 'no' for an answer as he escorted her to their bedroom. Jenny had taken her boys off earlier. Peter got up and shuffled to his room. The men cleaned up the bottles and other debris. Michael went outside to get some fresh air. Jerry was already there, in the open air, smoking a cigarette. He was looking into the nighttime sky. He noticed Michael and waved him over.

Jerry pointed to the sky. "Will you look at that? I never get tired of seeing all those stars."

Michael looked up at the black sky filled with a sea of stars. "Amazing."

"Would you like a smoke?" Jerry asked.

"Sure." Michael took a cigarette. He lit it and began to smoke. He looked back at the stars. "Frankey and I used to stay up at night at our cabin on the lake and look at the stars. I've forgotten how beautiful they are."

Jerry kept looking up. "Yeah. Makes ya think. About all this."

They stood smoking their cigarettes in silence for a couple of minutes.

"Hey!" They turned and saw the rest of the men walking away from the lodge.

"We're going down to the shack." Matt beckoned to them. "Come along."

Michael turned to Jerry. "What's that?"

"Oh, it's our special place. Come. Have a quick look."

Michael yawned. The long day was beginning to catch up on him. Tiredness was rolling over him like a big wave. The sweat from dancing was starting to chill his body in the cold air.

Jerry grabbed his arm and gave him a tug. "Come on."

Michael sighed. "Okay, but I have to get to bed soon."

They followed the other men with their flashlights as they wound their way through the snow in the woods. All that could be heard was crunching of footsteps and a lonely owl hooting in the distance. After five minutes they arrived. There was no electricity in the shack, but the other men had already lit lamps and hung them up inside. It was a simple low building made out of the nearby pine. There was an open area with a table and chairs. Three worn, old sofas were set in a semi-circle. Michael entered and looked around. In the back, beyond the open area, he saw three bedrooms.

Two of the men were setting up the alcohol and Alex was sat at the table, chopping up a white pile of cocaine.

"Welcome to the shack." Matt took Michael by the arm and ushered him to the table. "Would you like a line?"

Michael looked at the cocaine, then at the surroundings and all the other men. "Sure. Why not?"

The men gathered around the table. Matt tightly rolled a ten-dollar bill, lent over, and snorted a long line of cocaine. "Whoa!" He shook his head vigorously. Then he handed the note to Jerry who took his turn. They all got in a line and took their turn snorting the coke. Bob put out shot glasses of tequila and they each grabbed a glass after the coke, throwing it into the back of their throats.

"Oh, yeah! Oh, yeah!" the men shouted as they slammed the empty glasses on the table and fist-pumped the air.

Michael did the cocaine and threw the tequila into the back of his throat. He halfheartedly threw his arm in the air as Jim slapped him on the back. He felt a little dizzy then a buzz go through his body. "Wow, that was quite a nightcap."

"Yeah," Jim said, taking a deeper sniff to make sure the coke stayed in. "It can get quite crazy in this little shack sometimes."

Michael watched the men line up for another cocaine/tequila cocktail.

"Another one?" Jim asked.

He was far too gone to resist. "Mmmmmm... Okay." Michael said and leaned over the table for another line. He took a deep sniff through the rolled bill and felt the cocaine attack the back of his nose. He declined the tequila.

"I'll drink yours for you!" Matt said and did in one quick shot.

Michael staggered around the room trying to regain his composure. He fell into one of the sofas next to Jerry. He looked around the room. "Quite a little place you have here." He then pointed to the bedrooms. "What I don't understand is... if you have such a comfortable lodge, why do you have bedrooms down here?"

Jerry's smile disappeared and he bobbed his head. "I think we need to have a little chat. Give me a minute." Jerry got up went over to Matt and spoke to him. Matt glanced at Michael then back at Jerry. He nodded to Jerry. The two came over to Michael and sat down. The other men were oblivious to the three and kept on partying.

Michael looked at the two men. He was floating on a tequila-cocaine high. "So, what's this about?"

"We have a saying here," Matt said, "that whatever happens at the lodge, stays at the lodge."

"But we're not so sure what we're going to tell you can just stay here," Jerry said.

Michael shook his head. "I don't understand."

Matt and Jerry turned to each other, then Jerry spoke. "This is our den of vice and pleasure. This is where we really let our hair, what is left of it, down."

All three seemed to take deep breath at the same time.

"We get women from the reservation to come here," Matt said.

Michael stared at them both. "I see..."

Matt squirmed in his seat but stared right at Michael. "Essentially it becomes a brothel. A few women come, we pay them and take them into the bedrooms."

Jerry put his hand to his face and stroked it. "So that is what the bedrooms are used for."

Michael peered down at the floor then up at the bedrooms. He looked at Matt and Jerry. "Did my brother use the women?"

"He did. Once in a while," Jerry said.

"But not often," Matt added.

Michael rubbed his hands together. "Well, I don't know what to say guys, I…"

Jerry put his hand up. "There is more."

"More?" Michael scrutinized them both.

The three sat in silence. The other men had done anther line of coke and shot of tequila. They were shouting and laughing loudly with each other.

Matt scrunched up his shoulders. He closed his eyes. He took a deep breath and blew out the words before he could stop them. "Children. Kids."

Michael stopped breathing. His jaw clamped shut.

Matt opened his eyes and repeated. "Children. Yes, kids were born out of these nights of debauchery in this shack."

"Oh, no," Michael said. He turned to the bedrooms then back

to the men. "How many? Where are they?"

Matt shifted uncomfortably on the sofa. "Well, we are not totally sure how many."

"What?" Michael shook his head. "You don't know…"

Jerry cut in. "We know of two for certain. Maybe more. Some of them who got pregnant lost them during pregnancy."

The other men were now dancing around the table and singing the words to 'Brown Sugar' by The Rolling Stones.

Michael sighed. "God, didn't you protect yourself? Didn't they?"

Matt gestured with his arms. "We did. They did. But things got pretty wild here sometimes. People lost control."

Jerry shook his head. "Yeah. We sure did. Lots of times."

"We said two for certain," Matt said. "To be honest, no one knows who the actual father is of one. But we are pretty certain we know who the father of that one is. A girl."

Michael looked straight ahead at the wall. "Who? Frankey?"

"No, no," Matt shook his head. "Your father."

Michael put his hands to his face. "Oh Christ," he muttered.

The others had quieted down as Matt caught their eye. Bob turned off the music. They all came over to stand at the back of the sofas.

"My dad," Michael murmured.

Jerry moved closer to Michael. He put his arm around him. Michael's body was stiff and moved away.

"Frankey has been supporting these kids. Paying the mothers," Alex blurted out. The others looked at him and told him to hush.

Michael looked up. "What?"

Alex was about to speak again but Matt raised his hand to be silent. He obeyed and hung his head.

"Yes," Matt said. "We've recently found out that your brother has been supporting these children. Giving money to the mothers."

"And my dad?"

Jerry pulled Michael into him. "He told me once he didn't want anything to do with them. He had paid already for their services."

"Yeah, that's right," Bob butted in. "We paid…"

"Shut the fuck up!" Matt growled.

The men all looked at each other. No one said a word.

Finally, Michael stood up and sighed. "Well, gentlemen, this has been quite a day." He turned to Jerry. "I'd like to see these kids. Especially my sister. Any chance of that?"

Jerry shrugged. "Not sure. I'll see what I can do."

Michaels's voice began to break. "No, I really want to see these kids."

Jerry nodded and put his hands up. "Okay, okay. I'll get ahold of Joe the chief on the reservation tomorrow morning."

"Good," Michael said. "I want to bring my sisters too. And my dad. If he wants to come."

Jerry and Matt both nodded. "Okay."

Michael then looked at them all. "Good night, men."

Jerry jumped up. "I'll walk you back to the lodge."

"No, thanks." Michael half smiled. "I just need a long walk and to be alone right now."

He turned and walked out of the shack into the night. He looked up into the vast starry sky and wished he could just disappear into it.

Chapter 22

An hour later, Michael stumbled back into the lodge. The mixture of alcohol, cocaine and adrenaline was beginning to leave his body. He took his shoes off and tiptoed into the room. The last thing he wanted right now was to wake his father. He just wanted some peace. His clothes dropped to the floor. He had no intention to hang them up or put them on the wooden shelves. The bed gave out a high-pitched squeak as he sat down on it. He glanced at his father. Peter was still. He cautiously lay down on the bed and pulled the heavy quilt over him. His head sunk into the pillow. The remainder of the cocaine in his system tried to stir his body, but intense fatigue was winning the battle. It would be only a matter of minutes before he would fall asleep.

"Did ya have a good time down there?" his father asked.

"Dad. Sorry, didn't mean to wake you."

"Wasn't sleeping." Peter rolled over in his bed. "Can't sleep."

The furnace down the hall emitted a low reassuring hum and filled the silence of the room.

Peter shook his quilt briskly. "Any of them make a pass at ya?"

"What?" Michael's body shook and he turned to his father.

Peter refused to look at him and continued to stare at the ceiling. "You know. A pass," he sneered. "Is that what you queers call it?"

Michael tuned onto his back. "Dad. I think you're still drunk.

Let's call it a night." Then he turned again and faced the wall. He pulled the quilt tightly to his neck and closed his eyes.

Peter ignored Michael's suggestion and persisted. "I always thought that Jim might be one. Even Jerry. I never thought of either one of them as being real guys. Too soft," Peter snorted. "I mean, look at the way ya all were dancing out there at the end," he muttered. "Bunch of fairies."

Michael opened his eyes and stared at the wall. "So that is what you think?"

"Yep, that is what I think." He looked at Michael's back. "Think I was proud of my son who wore tights and pranced around a stage? Well, I wasn't."

An uneasy silence, like one before a storm, filled the room.

Michael sighed. "Sorry to have disappointed you."

"Well, you did," his father shot back. "Frankey made up for you, though."

Michael's body tensed with rage. He flipped over and stared through the darkness at his father.

"So, Dad. It sounds like you had some fun at the shack yourself."

The furnace continued to rumble on.

"Oh, they told you," Peter snarled. "They couldn't keep their fucking mouths shut. Bastards." Peter rustled his quilt, shook his legs. He chuckled. "Yeah, it was fun. Those Indian women know how to please a man. You should try it sometime. Might change you."

Michael sat up in his bed. "No, Dad, I don't think that is possible." He laid back down again. "And so I hear you have at least one more daughter and maybe even a grandson."

Peter brought his knees up in bed. "Don't know anything about that." He made a fake yawn. "I think it's time we stop talking. Think we have said enough."

"Dad. I think..."

Peter interrupted him and growled. "I said no more talking. I'm tired. Goodnight."

Michael didn't reply. He just stared at the ceiling. After a few minutes he gathered his quilt and pillow and left the room. He found a sofa to sleep on in the living room. He listened to the furnace but its warmth gave him little comfort.

Chapter 23

Morning came quickly. The smell of sizzling bacon, toast and coffee pervaded the lodge. The dog moved from group to group, wagging his tail, picking up scraps thrown to him, getting an endless breakfast. People sat around the table and spoke in hushed tones. All were nursing hangovers.

Michael found Mary outside, smoking a cigarette with Gina.

Gina looked at him and blew her cigarette smoke into the air. "Jesus, Uncle. I'd say look what the dog dragged in, but I don't think even a dog would have anything to do with you."

Mary scanned him up and down. "You do look a bit rough, brother. You okay?"

"Yeah, not much sleep." He rustled his hair. "Stayed up with the boys down in a shack they have in the woods. Could I get one of those?" He pointed to the cigarette.

"Sure," Gina said.

Michael lit the cigarette. "Thanks." He inhaled deeply, coughed then blew the smoke out above him.

Mary shook her head. "You sure you're okay?"

Michael turned to Gina. "I really need to speak to Mary in private for a few minutes. Sorry. Is that okay?"

Gina hastily stubbed her cigarette out. "That's fine, Uncle Mike. Getting kind of cold out here, anyway. I'll go get some toast." She shuffled back to the lodge.

"I'll be in in a minute," Mary called out to her as she left. Mary took one more puff of her cigarette and threw it into the nearby snow bank. "What's up, Mickey?"

Michael pulled out the little red Indian doll. "Remember this?"

Mary stared at him. "Go on."

"The doll represents children that were born and living on the reservation. We have a sister and possibly a nephew."

"Oh my God!" Mary gasped. "Dad? Frankey?"

Michael threw his cigarette down and held her. "Yes."

"Oh, no," Mary muttered.

"Frankey was giving them money. Supporting them." He stroked her head. "I've arranged to go see the mothers and the children now before the service," Michael said.

Mary sighed then broke away from him and dried her tears. "Fine. Let's do it. I'll get Anne and I'll meet you at the car. Is Dad coming?"

"No," Michael replied.

Mary rushed into the lodge. She didn't notice Gina standing there with two coffee cups.

"So can someone please tell me where we are going?" Anne asked from the backseat of the car. "I thought the service was this morning?"

Mary turned around from the front seat. "It's not till midday. Some local people want to attend."

Anne leaned forward and clung onto the front seat. "Okay... I'm still in the dark as to where—"

Mary cut in. "Michael. Are you going to tell her what you told me this morning or should I?"

Michael sighed, then found a place to pull over. Just ahead was a plowed lay-by. He pulled in, stopped the car and turned off the engine. Mary moved closer to him. He turned around to face

Anne. "Anne, we are going to meet our half-sister and possibly our nephew."

Anne's mouth fell open. "What the hell!" Her eyes darted between the both of them, "What? Where?"

Mary took her hand. "At the Indian reservation. About five miles away."

"Really? Huh." Anne's head turned away and pulled back from Mary's grasp. She slouched back into the seat and closed her eyes.

Michael leaned over the backseat and reached out to touch her. "Anne?"

Anne opened her eyes and bolted upright. She leaned over to her purse and opened it. "Well, that explains this thing, then." Out of her purse she pulled out a little red Indian doll.

Mary fiddled with her purse and pulled an identical doll and showed it to Anne. "We all got one. Even Dad."

Anne fondled the doll. "You said half-sister, maybe nephew. Dad? Frankey? How do you know this?"

Michael spoke. "Last night, after you all went to bed, I walked down with the men to another building. A large shack is hidden deep in the woods. No road to it. No electricity. Just a simple winding path. After some more drink and drugs they told me what they got up to there. Over the years these men brought women from the reservation for their pleasure. And, out of those nights of debauchery, children were born. It is uncertain exactly who the fathers are, but for certain Dad is the father to one of them, possibly Frankey to another."

"Oh, God," Anne murmured.

They all leaned into each other and gave each other a long embrace. Both Anne and Mary started to cry. They were oblivious to the cars and trucks that roared by. At a quick glance, they resembled lovers in a passionate embrace. A few of the vehicles honked their horns as they passed by.

As they disentangled, Michael dried his eyes too. "Mary, why don't you get in the back with our sister?"

Anne shook her head. "No, you two are close. I'll be okay back here." She pulled out some tissue and dried her eyes and blew her nose.

"Nonsense. I'm coming." Mary got out of the front seat, slammed the door and got into the back. She and Anne immediately embraced.

"Well, you were always Mama's favorite. The rest of us had to do something to survive," Mary kidded Anne as they snuggled.

Anne giggled. "Yes, I guess I was." She glanced at Mary. "But I was still envious of you three. Especially how you kept close as you got older."

Michael turned around and started the car. "Well, we're here now. Together and close. Let's go see these kids." And he pulled out onto the highway.

The entrance to the reservation was down a narrow, snow-plowed road. The village consisted of a group of houses, all in need of repair, and rusty worn trailers. These were spread out in a clearing that was next to a large frozen lake. Dogs that had been sitting on the porches of the houses and trailers started to bark. Some made their way towards the car, stopping at a distance to continue to bark. Others just lay and watched.

Mary stroked her doll in the back seat. "Do you know where we are going?"

"Jerry said it was the green house on the left when you came into the village." Michael scanned the row of houses. "He said she would be expecting us."

They looked out and noticed almost all the houses were some shade of green.

An old Indian man wrapped in a long army coat and brown scarf stood by the road watching them. Smoke from his cigarette surrounded him. It made him look like a ghost. Michael drove up to him, stopped and rolled down his window.

Michael looked up at the stern-looking man. "Good morning. Could you tell us where Alice lives?"

The Indian stared at them. He leaned down and peered at Michael in the front. Then the two women in the back.

"You're not supposed to be here," he said.

Michael squirmed in his car seat. "Yes, we're aware of that, but Joe said we could make a brief visit."

The Indian continued to stare at them. "Did he now?" He took another drag of his cigarette and blew it out. He pointed to the second house on the left. "Over there."

Michael thanked him, rolled up the window, and pulled away. He drove towards Alice's house. The Indian stood motionless and continued to watch them.

Anne piped up from the backseat. "Who is Joe?"

Michael steered the car on icy road. "He is one of the elders here. Everyone considers him the chief." The car turned into Alice's short driveway and stopped. "Dad and all the men at the lodge know him."

"Did Dad set this up?" Anne asked. "Why isn't he here?"

A large German Shepherd sat up on the porch and came out towards them. The door from the house opened and a short woman appeared. She shouted at the dog. It stopped in its tracks and returned to the house.

Michael unfastened his seat belt. "Dad didn't set this up. He doesn't even know we're here. We spoke last night after I got back from the shack. He doesn't want anything to do with this."

Anne gazed at the woman and massaged her doll. "Huh. Typical."

Michael turned around and faced his sisters. "Joe knew about the children. He was the one who organized the Indian dolls being delivered one to each of us. And he knew it was Frankey who financially supported these children. None of the other men at the lodge or Dad were interested. Joe thought we could help."

"Oh my God," Anne murmured.

Mary swung open her door. "Well, let's see what we can do."

The three got out of the car and made their way to the house. The dog sat up again but the woman made him lay down immediately.

"Alice?" Michael asked as they came to the door.

She bit her lip as all three stood smiling at her. "Yes, hello." Alice tentatively extended her hand. They all eagerly stepped up and shook it. "And you're Frankey's brother and sisters? I wasn't sure exactly who was coming."

Mary nodded. "Yes we are."

She opened the front door. "Welcome. Please come in."

The house inside was dark and simple. But it was clean and well kept. The kitchen and living space was one large room. There was one dull ceiling light in the middle of the room, with three other low side lights scattered throughout. A large fireplace with a lit pile of logs occupied one side of the room. A series of bright local landscape paintings, in different sizes with crude handmade frames, covered the walls. A bathroom and two bedrooms were connected at the back. Alice pointed to the worn brown sofa and chairs. "Please, have a seat."

They all took furtive glances around the room as they sat

down. Mary and Anne put their dolls away.

Anne spoke. "Thank you for having us at such short notice."

Alice stood in front of them with her hands folded. She nodded in acknowledgement. "Would you like some coffee? I've made some already."

Alice was in her late forties, short but strong and sturdy. She was wrapped up in two sweaters and a scarf. The fireplace threw out a weak heat.

Mary jumped up. "Oh, if it's not too much trouble. I'll help." Mary hurried across the room to where the kitchen was.

While Alice and Mary prepared the coffee, Michael stood up and went over to the paintings. He examined each of the paintings carefully. He turned to Alice. "Gosh, these are really good. Did you do them?"

Alice blushed. "Yes. They're not very good. But I like to paint."

Michael turned to the paintings again. "No. No. They are actually very good. Look at this flat perspective. The simple but strong trees. The bold color. They're folk art. Like that famous Canadian artist, Maud Lewis. She…"

"Michael," Mary snapped. "We don't need an art history lesson right now."

Michael stopped and swiveled around. "Oh, sorry," he said and he inched back to the sofa. "But they are really good," he blurted out, as he sat down with his coffee.

Alice smiled to herself as she sat down. "Thank you."

They sipped their coffee in silence.

Finally, Alice spoke. "I'm so sorry to hear about Frankey. It was such a shock to us all. He was such a nice man."

Michael nodded. "He was. When did he start coming here, contacting you?"

"He first came just over a year ago. On Sherry's birthday. He brought a present for her. He came with Joe. He introduced himself, but I could see he was related to Peter."

Anne leaned forward. "Yes, they do look very similar. Many people said he should have been named Peter Jr."

"He came back a couple of days later and said he wanted to help pay for Sherry's upbringing."

"So…" Michael gripped his coffee cup. "I hate to ask… but is Frankey her father?"

Anne and Mary scornfully looked at him. "Michael!"

Alice put her hands up. "No, no. It's okay. It really is. Peter is her father. No question."

Mary put her coffee down. "Well, now that we know that," she sent another dagger towards Michael, "we would like to take over for Frankey. Contribute financially to Sherry's upbringing."

The door from the bedroom opened and a voice came from it. "Mommy?"

They all turned to the door, and they saw a tall, thin girl with long black hair. She was about fourteen years old and dressed in a bathrobe. She looked like an Indian version of Mary; the eyes, nose, and jaw.

Alice stood up. "Sherry. You're awake."

The girl stood at the door.

Alice beckoned to her. "Come here darling. These are Frankey's brother and sisters."

She hesitated, then shuffled her way to her mother and they sat down together. Sherry nervously glanced at the three.

Mary half reached out towards her. "Hello, Sherry."

Sherry drew in closer to her mother.

Anne spoke. "Sherry. We didn't know till a few hours ago that you're part of our family. We wanted to meet you."

Mary stayed leaning forward. "Sherry. You and all of us share the same father. Frankey, too. We are your sisters and brother."

"Old sisters and brother," Michael smiled. "But family nonetheless. Welcome."

Alice wrapped he arms around her daughter. "She has been very upset about Frankey."

"Mom…" they heard her say into her mother's chest.

The wood in the fireplace crackled and a flame leaped from log to log as the fire began to ignite. It startled the dog and she got up and moved away from the flames to Alice's feet.

Anne reached for her purse and coat. "Maybe this is all a bit much to take in right now."

"Yes." Michael started to stand. "Maybe we can do this another time."

"No. Please stay a little longer. You have come out here to meet us," Alice said. "And some of you live so far away."

They all resettled in their places.

"These two live quite far away," Anne said. "But I'm fairly close. In Minneapolis. And I have a daughter a couple of years older than you. Maybe you could come and meet her some time."

Alice coaxed her daughter. "That would be nice."

Sherry nodded and sat up.

"I live in Florida. By the beach. It is sunny and warm there all the time. Have you ever seen the ocean?" Mary asked.

Sherry shook her head.

"Neither have I!" Anne said.

"And, of course, you'll have to come to London and have tea with the queen and me," Michael said, jokingly.

Sherry leaned into her mother. "Does everyone talk like him over there?"

Alice gently shook her daughter. "Sherry…"

Mary put on an English accent. "Actually, they do. I have been over to visit a few times. They all sound so sophisticated." Then she went back to her normal accent. "But most of them are very ordinary. Don't be fooled by Michael."

Anne picked at a loose thread on her coat. "Well, maybe we should start with Minneapolis first and take it from there."

Michael looked at his watch. "Well, actually. We have to be going. There is the ceremony for Frankey in just over an hour and we need to make another visit here."

Mary turned to Alice. "I hope you can come to the ceremony. It is at the lodge. We still have half his ashes."

"Yes, we are coming. We would be honored."

They all stood and shook hands. Mary and Anne broke the handshakes and gave Alice and Sherry long, deep hugs.

Michael took Alice aside. "And we will take over the money side that Frankey was helping with."

"Thank you," Alice said, "but let me be clear." She looked them all in the eye. "We are not a charity. I have a job and can take care of my daughter and myself. Frankey and I decided that the help would come in the form of a trust for Sherry's university education. She would like to study to become a veterinarian."

"We'll definitely help." Michael looked at the paintings. "I'll tell you what. How about if I buy one of those paintings?"

Mary shook her finger. "Michael!"

"Oh, shush, sister! I know good art when I see it." He grinned at Sherry. "See what sisters are like? Nag, nag, nag. I hope you're not going to be like that."

Sherry blushed crimson red.

Alice put her hand to her mouth. "Oh, I couldn't ask for anything. Which one would you like?"

"Oh, I love them all." He pointed to one. "But that one is my favorite." He pointed to the smallest of the paintings. It was of an Indian girl standing by a lake at nighttime.

Alice went over and took it off the wall and gave it to him.

Michael studied it then embraced the painting. "Thank you. I'll treasure it."

Anne started to move towards the door. "Sorry we must go."

Mary and Anne had already passed through the door when Michael stopped. "Oh. Can you tell me where Rachael lives?"

Alice gestured, "Further down. Closer to the lake. The second trailer from the end."

With that, the three left for the car. Alice, Sherry and the dog stood together on the porch. As they made their final waves and got into the car, Alice shouted out, "Michael!" And she hurried towards them.

Michael moved to meet her. "Yes?"

Alice drew Michael in close. "I think you should know that Rachael's child is not your father's or Frankey's. It is either Bob's or Matt's. Frankey knew this but still helped her out."

Michael scratched his head. "O, thanks. I guess we will too." They smiled and hugged each other then they separated.

When he got into the car, Anne asked, "What was that?"

Michael started the car and pulled the car out of the driveway. "She wanted to give me the title of the painting. It's called Sherry's Dream."

Alice and her daughter continued to stand on the porch and watched while the three entered Rachael's home. Then they and the dog went back into their house.

Chapter 24

"Let's get started," Jim said.

The men from the lodge stood in a semi-circle, with the urn of Frankey's ashes on a low table in front of them. The family and local people stood on the other side. The sky was silver-grey as the sun tried to push through the thin winter cloud. A dry, cold wind whistled through the trees.

"Frankey was our leader and a true friend," Jim began.

The sound of a vehicle could be heard coming in off the main road. An old battered pick-up truck came into driveway and parked up. Joe, Alice, Sherry and Rachael got out of the truck and looked over at the group.

Peter leaned into Michael and muttered, "Oh, Christ. Suppose you invited them."

"You hush," Anne snarled at her father.

Peter backed off.

Jim waved at them and shouted out, "Hello! Please come and join us! We've just started!"

The men from the lodge glanced at each other, then at their feet. They began to move from one foot to another, scratching at the snow-covered ground. The four made their way over to the group. Alice, Jenny, and Rachael locked arms as they walked. Joe shuffled behind them with his hands deep into the pockets of his long winter coat. Jenny shivered from the cold and brought her two boys closer to her for warmth as well as comfort. The four Indians joined the assembled group.

"Well as I said," Jim began again. "He was our leader, our friend. We have decided that each of us from the lodge should come up with a word that best describes him. Once said, we will scatter a bit of his ashes, here on our land. His land." He turned to Matt, "Matt will start."

Matt stepped forward, scooped out a ladle full of ashes. "Brave," he said, then spread the ashes under a nearby pine.

"Compassionate," Jim said, as he dropped the ashes to the ground.

"Wise," Jerry choked as he tried to hold back his tears.

"Honest," Bob gravely murmured.

"Stubborn-as-an-old-mule," Harry shouted out to a chorus of laughter.

Finally, Alex came forward. "If Harry is cheating, so am I," he took a deep breath. "You-were-a-much-better-man-than-me." Then he spread the ashes at the base of a stump. Tears sat in his eyes.

When Alex finished, Jim walked and stood over the urn. "There are a few ashes left. Would anyone else want to scatter?"

Jenny looked down and pulled her boys even tighter to herself. Everyone else stood motionless.

Alice took two small steps then strode forward and stood in front of Jim. "May I?" He glanced at the other men, then nodded.

Alice took the urn and began walking towards the woods. Rachel moved quickly to get by her side. Joe held Sherry's hand and followed.

"What the…" Peter started but stopped.

The group watched the women, then dutifully followed in a line through the snow. After a short time, they could hear the sound of moving water. Alice and Rachael came to it and stopped at the small stream. The rest came up and huddled together. Alice and Rachael stood apart from the group. They closed their eyes. Rachael brought out a small drum and began to slowly beat on it. Alice began to chant in a high singing tone. After a minute, Rachael joined in, an octave lower. Their feet, in old, worn boots, stomped rhythmically in the snow. The beautiful chanting got louder and filled the woods. Michael could feel his whole body tingling and, glancing around, was sure everyone else was feeling the same. The chanting and beating came to a crescendo then suddenly stopped. There was a moment of clear, rarefied silence.

Alice opened her eyes. "I'm now going to pour Frankey's spirit into the stream. The waters will take it through the hunting land he loved, past all the birds and animals. The waters will then take his spirit to our land, past the people he respected and cared for. His spirit, through the waters, will then pour into larger rivers, finally emptying into the great river you call the Mississippi. There it will pass through where he was born and then all the way down to the gulf, and finally onto the great seas to spread him to all his family that live afar." Alice bent down and poured the ashes into the stream. The moving waters grabbed them and like a white ghost, they began their travels. The gathered watched as the ashes disappeared down the stream. They stood in prayer and silence. The tall pines swayed in the winter wind.

Chapter 25

Joe stood at the door of Peter's room at the lodge. "I thought that at the end of the ceremony you might come over and at least say hello."

Peter was packing his bag. He turned to Joe.

"Hi," he said. Then he returned to his packing.

Joe leaned against the door. "Your kids went out to the reservation this morning to meet their sister."

"Did they now?" Peter continued to pack.

"Yeah, they did." Joe took a step into the room. "Alice and Rachael said that they promised to continue to financially support their families."

Peter turned and scowled at Joe. "Continue paying? Who has been paying?" he muttered. "And they ain't family." He returned to his packing.

"Yeah, that's what I thought you'd say."

Peter dropped his clothes in his suitcase. "Well, if that's what you thought, then I'm not sure why you're here?"

The room became still, quiet.

"I'm here 'cause you lost your son," Joe stared at Peter. "You and I go way back. I remember when you first introduced me to your young son Frankey. I noticed how proud you were of that boy."

Peter hesitated. He stopped packing and sank to the bed. His shoulders slumped and his head flopped. After a few moments, he said, "Sorry, Joe." He peered up at Joe. "Yeah. He was a great son. Loved his hunting and fishing. Like me."

Joe moved closer. "I remember the time when he caught that big northern pike. It was almost as tall as him!"

Peter smiled. "Yeah, I remember that. That was some fish."

"He was a good man. We're all going to miss him. Saw him around at the reservation in the last year," Joe said.

Peter stroked his chin. "So he was paying them?"

"Yeah," Joe said.

Peter shook his head. "Huh."

Joe put his hand on Peter's shoulder. "None of the other guys in the lodge contributed or gave a damn," he said. "Your son was quiet and respectful. A solid man."

The two boys started to run up and down the stairs chasing each other. Jenny stood at the top of the stairs and shouted for them to stop. They stopped immediately, but quickly began again.

Peter watched the boys. "Frankey and Mikey were like those two. Always playing, horsing around. Never quiet."

"Yeah," Joe said. "Young boys have a lot of energy. I only had daughters. And they only had daughters. As I'm old, the granddaughters are sweet. Not so loud."

Peter chuckled. "Not my granddaughter. She came out loud and with attitude. Never changed."

Joe moved away and leaned on a nearby wall. "Yeah. People don't, do they? Change, that is."

A red ball followed by a racing dog and the two boys rushed past the room.

"So I was always a selfish, mean son of a bitch? Feeling sorry for myself?" Peter asked.

"Nah," Joe grinned. "You weren't always. When I first met you, and for many years, you were thoughtful and kind. Even to the ladies." Joe's face became serious. "Then something happened. You became gnarled and twisted like a mean old oak. Distant. What happened?"

"Life." Peter sighed. "I guess it wore me down." Peter unhurriedly stood up and stretched. "Got time for a little stroll?"

Joe began to button his coat. "Sure."

The two men walked through the lodge, past the people packing up to leave, and made their way out into the snowy wood. They walked side by side.

"I can't imagine losing one of my kids," Joe said.

Peter stared up at the trees. "It hurts. It hurts real deep."

Joe put his arm around Peter. Peter stuffed his hands deeper into his pockets.

"Losing Sally was hard," Peter said. "She didn't deserve what she got. Even though we drifted apart, like most couples do, I thought we'd have some years together when the kids had left. Then I wouldn't be so grumpy and tired with work. Maybe we'd get a new start. But it didn't happen. So when I stopped my job and went up north, I thought I would be able to spend more time with Frankey, fishing and hunting. The other kids and I never really hooked up. It was only Frankey. And now he is gone too."

Joe pulled Peter into him in a half hug then released him. They walked in silence. The sound of the stream rumbled in the distance.

"Well," Joe mused, "some great philosopher said, 'In life, shit happens'. It's what you do with that shit that counts."

Peter stopped and smirked. "Who the fuck said that?"

"Plato, the Greek philosopher. Or was it Pluto, the Disney dog?" Joe said with a twinkle in his eye.

"Sounds like Pluto to me," Peter grinned. He scratched his light beard. "But that makes sense. Guess I got a lot of shit right

147

now."

They began to walk again. Peter spoke. "You know, there is just no time in life. We had all that craziness of the war. Then we come home. We get a job, wife, kids, keep our heads down in an ass-tiring routine. Then we are spat out at the other end with aching joints, poor eyesight, and a dick that doesn't work anymore. And then on top of that, you lose the people you love the most in this life. None of this is making any sense to me anymore."

"Not sure what advice Pluto would give to that," Joe said. "Probably just try to keep moving. Don't get stuck."

Peter agreed. "Hmm… yeah, guess so."

Joe gently raised his arm. "And if you need a hand in shoveling that shit, I'm more than happy to help."

Peter peered at Joe. "Why you offering?"

"Well, you and me, we come from the same time. Just different places. Me from the reservation and you from the Iron Range. The war. It changed us. Even though we didn't fight day to day, we both saw and experienced a lot that people at home could never relate to. So we kept it in to ourselves and got on with our lives. But it was always there. Like an itch that never stopped itching. I ain't perfect. But I ain't bad either. I used those women too. But a while back I decided I'd try to help them a bit. So I did in my own little way. And you know, those women returned my care tenfold. We all care for each other now. Nothing special, just keeping an eye out and making sure everyone's life rolls along. So if I can, I'd like to help you a bit too."

Peter stared at him for moment. He turned and started to walk back to the lodge, Joe at his side. "I guess I'll get us a couple of those shovels. Make a start."

Chapter 26

Michael and Mary returned to Minneapolis after the funeral and stayed that night at a hotel in the airport. The next morning they would fly back to their respective homes.

Michael didn't wait for Mary to arrive to order his breakfast. He sat at a table by the window and watched the planes taking off. He could hear the engines bursting into life as the planes angled steep into the sky. A light flurry of snowflakes danced in the wind. Bacon, eggs and toast sat untouched on his plate.

"Better eat that before it gets cold," Mary said, as she slid in next to him.

Michael turned to her. "Oh, hi. Sleep okay?"

"God, I hate these airtight rooms with their pumped-in heating systems," Mary yawned. "I tossed and turned all night."

The waitress came over. "Would you like anything, ma'am?" Her dark eyes were attentive. The blue lettering on her badge read 'Mavis'.

"Mavis, I'd like a black coffee and one piece of toast."

"Coming right up." Mavis smiled and turned away.

Mary pulled out a cigarette and said, "Better service here."

"Well, the coffee is a bit weak," Michael started.

"Oh please, don't moan," Mary said. "As Grandma used to say, 'Shut up and eat'."

"Okay, okay." Michael stabbed at his bacon with his fork.

Mary lit a cigarette. She took a drag and blew it out, saying, "Spoke to Anne last night. She said Dad called her. They had a real heart to heart."

Michael continued to look at his meal. "Oh, really? I didn't know he had one."

Mary took another drag from her cigarette and blew it out the side of her mouth. "Oh, come on. Give Dad a break. Anne said that he was planning on doing something with Joe at the reservation. Didn't know what exactly, but something. To help out."

"Huh," was all that came out of Michael's mouth.

The waitress brought over the coffee and toast for Mary.

Mary harshly stubbed her cigarette out and leaned forward in her chair. "Listen. You're not the only one who is grieving here. We all are. I know you and Frankey were especially close growing up together. But you have to realize that Dad has lost a son. Man, neither one of us have had kids. Nothing can be worse than to lose your child. I know Frankey was a grown man. But to Dad he was still his kid. So quit feeling so sorry for yourself. You're not the only one who has lost someone."

Planes continued to take off, causing the windows to vibrate. A man's voice on the loudspeaker announced departures and gate numbers.

Mary put her hand on Michael's. "Sorry, Mikey. But I had to say that."

Michael squeezed it and smiled. "Shut up and eat," he said.

Shortly after, the boarding for London was announced. Mary and Michael strolled to the gate.

Michael put his arm around Mary. "Remember when Alice came to me at end of our visit? I said it was because she wanted me to know the title of the painting."

Mary gripped him hard. "Yes…"

"She wanted me to know that for certain neither Dad or

Frankey were the father of Jonny, Rachael's son."

"Really? Who is?" Mary asked.

"Alice said it could only have been either Bob or Matt. Frankey knew this but contributed nonetheless."

Mary playfully jostled his arm. "And so shall we! But why didn't you tell us?"

"Well…" Michael stalled. "I lost a brother, I didn't want to be the only boy in the family," he chuckled, "especially with all you girls."

Mary embraced him. "Oh, Michael. You softie. Fine. No one else needs to know. Jonny is family."

The final boarding call for London was announced. They held each other tight in front of the exit gate.

"Bye for now, little sister. Be well. Come and visit soon." Michael kept holding on to her.

"I will." She released her embrace. "You better go or you'll have to spend another day in this frozen tundra."

They parted and Michael strode to the departure gate. He stopped, turned and pulled the little red doll out of his pocket and waved it at her. He blew a final kiss to her, then entered the plane.

He stowed his luggage above his seat and was relieved to see that no one was sitting next to him. He would be able to stretch out and sleep on the flight back. The plane taxied, gained speed and began to lift up into the sky. Michael looked out onto the flat, snow-covered Minnesota terrain. "Goodbye," he whispered, and he closed his eyes.

Mary watched the plane till it disappeared into the clouds. She started to leave the international terminal to go to the domestic one to catch her flight. She saw her father standing, looking at the departure board. In his arm was a red jacket.

"Dad!" Mary called out, waving to him.

Peter's eyes went from the board to her. He looked bewildered.

Mary rushed over to him.

"Dad! When did you get here? Are you okay?"

"Did I miss him? I can't see his flight anywhere on the board," he said.

"Yes, you just missed him. He left about ten minutes ago." She looked at the red jacket, "What is that?"

Peter held it up. "Oh, it's Frankey's letter jacket. You know, from High School. I thought Mikey might want it. To remember him by."

"That's really nice, Dad. I'm sure we can send it. Take it to Anne's. She'll help you."

"Yeah. Maybe." Peter gazed at the floor. "But mainly I wanted to talk to him."

"Oh. That's a shame. I suppose you could phone him in a couple days. Anne can show you how to do that too. To call long distance." She looked her father still staring at the floor. "Is there anything in particular you wanted to say?"

Peter took a deep breath; his voice was beginning to crack. "Not sure what I was going to say. Things have always been complicated between us. You know that. I was really mean to him last night." He looked up at Mary. "I guess I just wanted to say that I was sorry." He hung his head again and clutched at the jacket.

Mary put arm around her father. They began to stroll out of the terminal.

"Well, you missed him now. But I can tell you, he'd love to hear from you sometime. He really would."

Peter pulled his daughter close him. "Thank you. I love all

of you. I just find all of this so damn confusing sometimes."

Mary held him tight. She saw an airport bar and steered him towards it. "Hey, it's midday and I still have an hour before my flight. Let's be naughty and have one more drink. For Frankey Buck."

Peter squeezed her arm. "That's the best thing I've heard today."

And they walked arm in arm into the bar.